SPELLS LIKE A WITCH

BETTINA M. JOHNSON

AQUA RAVEN PUBLISHING

Spells Like a Witch

ISBN: 979-8-9850697-5-4

Cover art by Bettina M. Johnson

Happy Birthday in heaven, Mom.
This one's for you.

CHAPTER 1

The hammock hanging between two oak trees in my yard was a cozy spot to nap with Lorcan, my fiancé. We'd worked hard in the garden until exhaustion claimed us both. Instead of heading into the house to shower off and catch a few winks, the lure of the striped cloth swaying gently in the breeze was too enticing to pass up. Even in mid-September, the humidity was always a threat in the South. However, today it was surprisingly low, and the declining bugs decided to not make a meal of our arms and legs. Therefore, we opted for our outdoor bed, exposing us to the elements.

"Look. They're doing it in public now for everyone to see. Shameless."

Adriana. She was the elements.

My batty great-grandmother, a formidable dark witch, was addressing someone unknown to me.

"Now, Annie. Stop being a wicked witch. Those children are taking a nap. They look plumb tired, and that hammock makes a comfy resting spot."

Susanne Washington. She is my granny's best friend and

director of the choir at the local AME church—along with The Keeper of Tomes—a lofty title for someone who holds the key to The Forbidden Library. It's an underground lair of ill repute containing all manner of nasty books that would bite you if you looked at them wrong.

I could feel Lorcan sighing and knew he was awake.

"Well, if you look at where Lorcan is resting his hand, I'd say it was a fine spot—for getting away with public canoodling!" cried Adriana.

Lorcan quickly jumped up, rolled away, and stood, leaving me swaying and hanging onto the sides of the fabric. I was in danger of getting thrown off balance and spinning until I'd wind up wrapped like a mummy.

Belatedly, Lorcan realized what he'd done and turned to steady me, allowing me to sit up.

Good man.

"What do you want?" I spat at Adriana like a feisty demon, which I'm sure I resembled. I managed to stand up without spinning the earth off its axis and scowled at my great-grandmother.

Turning to the other woman, I sweetened my voice, "Hello, Susanne. How are you, ma'am?"

Now, with Susanne, I could be nice and remain polite. The dear older woman always had a twinkle in her eye and a kind word for yours truly. Me and granny, not so much. I'm sure oil and vinegar mixed better than the two of us.

Some would say it's because we are so alike.

Some should mind their own business before I minded it for them.

Heaving a sigh like the weight of the world was on her shoulders, Adriana pointed a gnarled finger in my direction.

"I need your cat."

"Why?"

"Why, what?"

2

Grr.

"Why do you need my cat?"

"What do you mean?"

Seriously?

"What do you mean, what do I mean? You come here, startle us out of a nap...and *only* a nap, mind you, ask for my cat...then start with this...this...whatever it is you do with me, again!"

"I'm not doing anything with you!" sniffed Adriana.

"Then why do you need my cat?"

"I have mice?"

"Try again."

I crossed my arms and waited for an explanation, knowing my granny might hem and haw. But eventually, she'd tell why she was here.

"I need Wicked to spy on someone for me."

There. Was that so difficult?

"Who? What's going on?"

"Who said anything is going on?"

I rolled my eyes and stomped past Lorcan, leaving Adriana and Susanne to hurry after me as I climbed the porch and slammed through my back door and into the kitchen. I turned on the coffeemaker and had grabbed my favorite mug by the time Adriana and Susanne caught up to me...Lorcan trailed behind with a bemused smile on his face.

"She's over there. I'm done." Pointing to my cat, sleeping in her favorite sunspot, I stomped into the den and picked up the book I'd been reading. I didn't care one bit about whatever drama Adriana had cooked up that needed said feline.

Lorcan came over and sat beside me, squeezing my knee in sympathy. He pulled a pine cone out of my hair, showed it to me, then kissed my cheek. Then he tucked it into his front shirt pocket before taking his phone out to check for messages. Of course, knowing Lor, that pine cone would go in his "things I shared with Lily" box—which was already jam-packed with knickknacks.

He'd spent the better part of the week working at his mechanic shop and volunteering. That Lor helped several of the men in town set up the decorations and build the structures needed for the upcoming Fall Festival notwithstanding, Lorcan then chose to help me all weekend with yard work.

"Don't ignore me, cat. I demand that you pay attention!"

Heh. Fat chance, that.

The town was in full preparation mode, and Lorcan was in the thick of it as much as he could afford to be. I knew most of the folks who ran businesses catering to the tourist crowd were giddy with anticipation of a profitable autumn. Even though we had one week left in August, the Halloween season started early in Sweet Briar, Georgia. I was undoubtedly excited.

Even those who had no business messing with the tourists—case in point, funeral director Hester Soule—had brewed a pumpkin-spiced something or other. Hester shared it with the construction crew, telling everyone she'd acquired a potent spice combination and created a masterpiece.

My dad, Charlie, raved at the taste and shocked us when he said Hermione Winters even sampled a bit.

The Winters sisters, with their tea shop across from the funeral parlor, were hardly on friendly terms with Chester and Hester. Hester's pumpkin-spiced brew must pack quite a wallop for that bridge to be crossed.

Lorcan said the peace offering dissolved when my cousin Nora turned up her nose at a sample while accompanying the Dietrich clan. They were making the rounds, complaining about every little decoration placement. Hermione offered our hated enemies a tasting of her tea, and Hester accused her of trying to steal customers.

Customers? It's not like Hester has a tea shop! She works with dead people all day!

After that disturbing thought, Lorcan declined a taste, and I knew he'd regretted it since he came home with pumpkin-flavored creamer for us to try.

The smell of brewing coffee filled the room, making my nose twitch. Time for a cup.

"I need you to tell me exactly what you saw."

"Mreow."

"No. Not in cat speak. In people speak."

"Mroo?"

"People speak!"

"Meow!"

Oh, this was going well. I dared risk a glance in the direction of Adriana's ridiculously one-sided conversation with Wicked, convinced my great-grandmother had finally gone off the rails of insanity. In fact, she nosedived off its edge without a parachute.

"Maybe someone will finally allow me to bring in a psychiatrist and get her some stronger meds than I suspect she's on," I loudly whispered to Lorcan. "It's cruel and unusual punishment to have her go on so. For us, that is."

Lorcan patted my leg, then stood, heading for the kitchen to play barista. Gosh, I loved a man who made me coffee without asking! And look—pumpkin creamer!

"This cat is a fraud." Adriana strode into the den with Susanne tugging on her blouse, trying to get a word in. Wicked, now sitting up and looking bored, blinked, then stretched. She didn't seem bothered by the proclamation regarding her trustworthiness.

"Woman! Would you stop messing with my top!"

"If you'd let me catch my breath and speak, I think I could clarify a few things with the young'uns," said Susanne.

I assumed Susanne was referring to Lorcan and me.

"Like you can make sense of what that insufferable busy-body has been spouting!"

Busybody?

Only one person in town could raise that much malice in Adriana. Petunia Macallister-Buchannon, the long-suffering, tongue-wagging wife of Bud Buchannon, a contractor and the man who'd renovated my home.

"What has Petunia been saying now?" I asked, noting with some satisfaction that Adriana acknowledged I'd correctly pinned the gossip with raised eyebrows and a smirk in Susanne's direction.

Lorcan returned with a tray and placed a mug in front of Susanne and Adriana. He then poured me a cup from the carafe, doctoring it with the spicy stuff...and a heap of sugar. Then, stirring idly, I sat back to listen to whatever nonsense Adriana had come to tell us.

"Just let *me* explain," said Susanne.

"You have the floor," said Adriana, who'd stiffly walked over to the chair opposite mine and sat. Her back was ramrod straight, and she wouldn't look at us, instead examining an imaginary thread on her sleeve. However, I noticed she'd inched her mug closer.

I tried to cut my grandmother some slack. After all, she'd been recently attacked by a deranged witch—my family seems to be a magnet for them. Adriana flourished in the care of clerics for a time until she'd made a remarkable recovery. Even after that, however, they insisted she take it easy for a few months until at least November. This did not sit well with her.

I'd noticed a weariness of late that kept me concerned, however. After all, Adriana was no spring chicken. But right now, I was losing patience faster than folks at an antique show listening to an auctioneer with a speech impediment.

Susanne turned to address us and suddenly looked self-conscious. She began patting her hair and straightening the crocheted yellow sweater she wore despite the mild day.

"Now, you have to take what I say with a grain of salt, but June wouldn't go off on a tangent for just any old thing. And Petunia might be a bigmouth, but she doesn't go around saying something unless there is a grain of truth."

June?

"What's up with June?" I asked, my interest suddenly piqued.

"Our dear friend insists Wicked paid her a visit and...well..."

"Spit it out, woman!" cried Adriana. "June is either losing her mind, or your cat can talk. June swore up and down she heard Wicked tell her something was wrong with Dennis, and she needs to investigate."

Oh ho! Proof!

I turned and glared at my cat, who proceeded to wash her nether regions. I chose not to bother addressing Wicked, knowing it would be a lesson in futility. Instead, I returned to the more pressing matter at hand.

A few of us knew this was coming. Ever since my early days arriving in Sweet Briar, I'd known something was going on as far as Dennis Carter was concerned. And if I had to guess, it had something to do with Rita Chase...the town herbalist and owner of a metaphysical shop. Rita was Brian's mom—my former beau—who is a police detective with the state.

I did *not* need this right now.

"Go on," I said.

What is wrong with me? Didn't I just claim I had no need for this drama?

"Dennis has been acting very strange as of late. Coming and going at all odd hours. June is beside herself with worry. When she questioned him, he said he'd had trouble sleeping and needed a walk...and so has...um." Susanne stopped speaking, cutting her eyes instead toward Adriana.

And so has...who?

I opened my mouth to ask, but Susanne coughed nervously and continued.

"Adriana thought perhaps if we came and spoke with Wicked, she might enlighten us," Susanne finished, turning again to face my black furball. Wicked continued to find her rear end highly fascinating.

"What do you have to say for yourself, young lady? You know she can speak plainly as day, although I tend to hear her in my head." This I addressed to the room at large. "Even though some people doubted me when I mentioned it."

I gave Lorcan a pointed look which he ignored and began fidgeting with his phone.

Odd that Dennis claimed to be hearing voices. Although, who am I to doubt? Wicked seems to be hellbent on making me look like a crazed woman despite my claims to the contrary. Maybe with June stating she'd heard her I wouldn't look so insane.

Maybe.

"Are you thinking it's Rita? Do you think they're doing the horizontal mambo?" asked Adriana. "The old sideways hustle? The slip and slide of love? Or in their case...lust?"

It seems Adriana and I are on the same wavelength. We'd all wondered the same thing about Dennis and Rita.

"OK! Enough euphemisms, please!" I cried. "You know I suspected them of some kind of shenanigans. I thought that was in the past, however. Dennis has been a devoted husband as of late...and Rita has been keeping her distance."

"Something is bothering Dennis. And before I confront him...and others, I want to make sure it's not something as simple as an affair," sniffed Adriana.

Confusion wrinkled my brow. What are we talking about if not an affair?

"Others? You don't think this is only about Rita and Dennis?"

Well, they certainly had been seeing a lot of each other. But something sinister is happening in this town, so you need to quickly ask some questions.

I jumped and spun around to find Wicked gone even though I'd received her message loud and clear. I turned to my guests, but no one reacted the same as me...so I knew I was the only one who'd heard the lousy beast. Adriana just nodded, but not because she heard my cat...it was in response to my question.

"Will you answer any more questions before I head out?" I asked Adriana.

"I'd rather wait and see what you discover with the Dennis and Rita situation first," she replied.

I breathed in, slowly counting to ten before letting out a vast amount of air, then began rubbing my temples in defeat.

"I'm on it."

CHAPTER 2

$\mathcal{T}$he dynamics of friendships have shifted around me as of late. Pandora decided to assist my cousins, Maggie and Ellie. She was currently traveling with their troupe and out of my hair. Although, if I had to admit it, I missed my crossroad demon friend.

Andrea was still attending college, and I hadn't seen much of her lately, nor her brother Steve, who was incredibly busy at the bakery.

Molly Hogan, my dear friend from my former life before discovering I was a witch, had moved back home to live with her mom and save some pennies. This had Brian moping around town. I knew they were sweet on each other but didn't know how far things had progressed with them—her untimely move back to Asheville, while close enough for weekend visits, had indeed put a damper on any love life they may have been kindling. She promised it wouldn't be a long exodus...but I missed her and had lost a competent employee to man my booth at the fairgrounds.

My book club buddies, Keisha, Martha, and Becky, were all busy with work—Keisha as a personal nurse to my great-grandfather, Antonio, Martha as the terribly efficient head librarian in town, and Becky who ran her own bookshop on the square. Becky's free time usually involved spending as much of it with Jake Carter, her boyfriend—Dennis and June Carter's son.

That's where I was heading this morning—to Jake's office a block off the town square. I had the unenviable task of questioning him about his parents' marital status. I sorely wished I had someone to tag along with me, which was why I about whimpered in gratitude when Edith Plank popped into the front seat of my Jeep.

"Edith! How nice to see you! Where have you been? I haven't seen you in ages!" I cried.

"Lily. I spent the entire summer getting under your nerves—your words—and finally decided to take a trip to visit friends in Florida. So it's not like I've been gone that long."

"I'm just glad to see you!"

Wait. Friends? Florida? Edith is a ghost. I didn't realize ghosts could mingle with others of their kind and travel. I carefully looked around, half expecting to see other spirits materialize around town and wave as we passed them. Thankfully, no other spooks were out and about that I could see.

"You have friends?" I blurted. "Ghost friends?"

"Oh, that's nice. Thanks," said Edith dryly. "Of course I have friends. A friend. One."

Edith became cagey, and I wondered at the change in her demeanor and instantly became suspicious.

"Edith, who's your friend?"

"Oh...um. Just someone from town who moved to Florida recently. It's nothing. Anyway...I'm assuming you've heard about Dennis and June Carter?"

"Edith..."

"Wicked told me something disturbing about the two, and I think you need to investigate further."

"Edith..."

"I mean...we all knew something was up with Dennis, and if he is about to hurt June, she should know before..."

"Edith Plank! You are avoiding my question, and I won't stop until you answer me. I might not have caught on if you had a better poker face. Who is your friend?"

"Just a guy I met who failed to move on...and eventually moved back home after he died. We've gotten friendly and might be dating. It's no big deal."

For a minute I felt horror course through my body. A ghost? In town? Here? Who failed to move on?

"You aren't dating Old Greg! Edith! How could you?"

"What? Lily, seriously? How could you even ask that?" cried Edith.

"But if not Old Greg, then..."

As thoughts ran wildly through my mind, I considered who it might be. Owen Crawley? The man who'd died when Mortimer and my Grandpa Antonio scouted the woods? And Antonio fell into the entrance of the underground prison— and into the clutches of the deranged Donna? Had he remained behind? The only other ghost as of late came crashing through the fog, and I shrank back in disgust and dismay.

"Gordon? Deputy Gordon Delaney?"

"It's not like that, Lily. Gordon changed!"

"He's evil! The man was out to get me! For heaven's sake, Edith...he dated Nora!"

I was aghast and disheartened at the prospect of Edith lowering herself to be with such a man. Even in ghost form, I couldn't see how Gordon Delaney could be any sort of pleasant being to be around. What caused Edith to see him in any other light? Was it just loneliness?

Trying to muster up some compassion for her plight, I still felt disappointment and apprehension that she'd cavorted with an enemy. Choosing to forget for the moment that Edith had, at one time, also been an enemy, I tried to put myself in her shoes—and failed.

"I can't believe you'd do this to me!" I wailed.

"Me? Do this to you? Lily Sweet! You have no right to tell me who I can spend time with! What kind of friend are you?"

"One who obviously thought you had better taste...and was loyal," I spat back, instantly regretting my words. Especially when I saw the hurt on Edith's face.

Did I apologize?

No.

Is that petty of me?

Yes.

Did Edith fade away to lick her wounds and leave me wondering what gossip she had learned?

You betcha.

Now I would never find out what gossip Edith heard. And why did my cat talk to her and not me? Or June for that matter? All this nonsense would be cleared up if that cat came to me first and told me the nitty-gritty.

Sighing at my now total complete loss of all friends for the foreseeable future and kicking myself for being such a hard-ass concerning Edith, I trudged onward toward Jake's office, hoping I'd manage to not alienate him at least. Otherwise, I'd have Lorcan, and only Lorcan, left as a friend...and even though that counted, he was my betrothed—so that seemed like cheating.

I mean, he had to like me!

Entering Jake's waiting room and dragging my feet to the reception desk, I noted the changes since I was there last. The most obvious was his new paralegal, who I assumed acted as receptionist as well, considering she was manning the phones while going over paperwork. I waited patiently, noting her nameplate. *Francine Willkie.*

Francine held up one finger with an apologetic smile for me and continued her conversation. This gave me time to study the woman. I put her in her midfifties, with just a hint of grey in her dark hair, bright blue eyes, plentiful laugh lines, and an assortment of items to keep her desk from being too impersonal.

I noted a bunch of kids' photos, and even those of a few pets along with an odd assortment of tiny gnomes and fairies on mushrooms and such—she even had a colorful betta fish in a bowl peeking out at me from his equally minuscule log.

All in all, I rather liked the woman without being properly introduced.

"I'm so sorry about that," she finally addressed me. These judges' assistants go on and on at me like I'm some kind of imbecile, and I'm stuck having to play nice. Now...you must be here to see Jake, only he's not expected back until 1:30 or so. Your name?"

"Lily Sweet. And I don't have an appointment...we're..."

"Friends. Yes...I know who you are. I just didn't know your face yet. Your name is rather famous around these parts."

Francine didn't recoil in fear nor look in askance at me from her safety position behind the desk—my wonky magic use usually precedes me—so I took that as a good sign. That meant she hadn't yet heard about my pathetic spellcasting ability or that I liked to live dangerously. That, or she wasn't a witch nor trusted with the knowledge.

I briefly wondered if we were related.

What? I seem to have relations all over the flipping state and beyond...so I felt justified in that particular train of thought.

"May I wait for Jake? I won't be a bother...unless he has afternoon appointments?"

"Oh, no, dear, go right ahead and wait. He'll be around shortly."

I didn't have to wait long. No sooner had I planted my behind in one of Jake's comfy armchairs than the man himself walked in, harried but smiling, until he saw me standing to greet him. Was that regret? Remorse? Fear? Something passed in those light baby blues to make me wonder if I'd done something to cause such a reaction.

"Lily! What are you doing here? Nothing serious, I hope?"

"Can't I stop by my friend's place of business out of the blue for a little chat?" I replied.

"Of course. But something tells me you are here for other reasons. Ones that I heard secondhand just now at the diner if I'm not mistaken."

He was probably on point.

"Can we head into your office?" I asked.

"Lead the way. Francine, hold my calls."

I didn't relish the thought of what the next few minutes would bring...but someone had to find out what was plaguing the Carter family...and I certainly wanted to prevent June from being hurt by whatever was going on. It was time to find out what that might be.

Hopefully, I wasn't too late.

CHAPTER 3

"Coffee? Tea?"

"No, Jake. Listen. I know you are busy. I'm not here for niceties, as you've guessed. It's just that..."

"You've been hearing the rumors about my dad around town," Jake said.

I sighed in relief that I didn't have to ask the awkward question, wondering if Jake was in the know. Obviously, he was.

"Oh, I'm so glad you know about it. I mean, it will be awkward enough talking to Rita," I said.

"Rita? Rita Chase? What does Rita have to do with what's going on with Dad?" Jake asked, a frown marring his good looks.

Oh no. What was Jake talking about that I had missed?

"Um...why don't you tell me why you've been worried, and I will fill you in on my end afterward," I asked.

Jake gave me a guarded expression, and I could see the wheels turning as he decided how to proceed, and what he deemed worthy of sharing. When he finally informed me, my boorish response belied his hesitation at telling me.

"Dad is hearing voices."

"*That's* the big secret? Voices?"

Jake stood and walked over to the window overlooking the street. I could tell by his stance I'd offended him.

"Jake. I'm sorry. I didn't mean for it to sound the way it did. That came out entirely wrong."

"I would think with your own dad suffering the same malady, you'd be more understanding, Lil."

Hang on. *My* dad?

"From the blank look on your face, I do believe we are here for different reasons," said Jake with a sigh. "Perhaps I better tell you what I know so far."

Sitting back down and steepling his fingers, Jake told me what was apparently ailing both our dads, and I was astounded to find out not only did I not know of this, but my parents had obviously kept it from not only me but Adriana as well.

"Our dads are hearing things. Voices, to be more specific. Often at night...that's when they both said it was common, they are awakened from a deep sleep by voices calling out to them. However, recently the voices started whispering softly during the day. It's not just our dads. Quite a few folks are reporting the same. I suspected no one informed you; otherwise, you'd have reached out to me by now."

"What are these voices saying?" I asked with some trepidation. I stuffed the hurt, putting my feelings aside temporarily as the knowledge I was one of the last to discover this voice-hearing phenomenon going around town.

"That's just it. So far, everyone suffering can't make out actual words. It's like they understand someone—or something—is trying to reach them, but the words sound as if they are stuttered and hollow. Echoing, if you will. Neither can make out what is being said."

"And why am I just finding this out? Adriana is going to be livid when she hears of this."

Jake remained solemn, not quite meeting my eyes.

"She already knows." It was a statement, not a question on my part.

"I tried to get Dad to speak to her...and you, which is why I'm not surprised you are here. Well, now I am—seeing as how you had no idea of the situation. So why are you here, Lily? What is this about Rita?"

I groaned inwardly, knowing there was no going back now. But perhaps this too, needed to be addressed.

"Rumors are going around town...well, gossip...it's just..."

I paused, looking chagrined and uncertain how to continue.

"Just spit it out, Lily," urged Jake.

"Some of us think Rita Chase and your dad might be having an affair."

There. I said it. Now I wanted the floor to open wide and swallow me whole.

However, Jake's reaction gave me pause. Was he crying? It was difficult to tell. His shoulders shaking and his face covered by his hand confused me until he threw his head back and laughed.

"Jake...seriously. Some of us have seen them skulking around town. Petunia Macallister-Buchannon has been blathering on about it. Heck, Lorcan and I even saw them in another county together, and they looked like they had a lover's quarrel," I argued.

Jake held up his hand, stopping any further protestation on my part. Then, wiping his eyes, he became somber, tugging at his bottom lip before explaining.

"It's not a laughing matter, really. It's just...I was reacting more to this blasted town and the Gossip Gang's penchant for spreading misinformation at every turn. No, Lily. I can assure you that my dad and Rita are not carrying on an illicit affair."

"But..."

"But nothing. Lily...Dad and Rita are brother and sister. Well, half anyway."

What?

"Did my mom ever tell you about my dad's people? My grandparents, Lula and Jeremy?" When I shook my head no, Jake began his sordid tale.

"My grandfather Jeremy was an evil man. A witch from the old school of thinking. That anyone not Breed was beneath him. Even some *in* the Breed did not pass muster. Jeremy and your ancestor, Lucretia, would have gotten along well. They were cut from the same cloth."

I shuddered just thinking about that vile woman.

"Cecelia Barrow was a human woman who lived nearby. Her family, entrusted with our secrets, found work in the witch hospital. Cecelia was psychic, so not far removed from our kind, but she had no magical talent to speak of. She was betrothed to a cleric, a fairly powerful witch, and this incensed Jeremy to no end, seeing as how he'd grown up with this man and considered him a close friend. That a talented cleric would throw his life away by marrying a mere human insulted his way of thinking."

Jake lowered his head, staring at nothing, and I guessed having such a vile relation was a blight on his family name. I know it disturbed my kin to have such in our own lineage.

"One day, he followed Cecelia home and, finding no one there, accosted her. He violated the poor girl, and Rita was the result. She only found out several months ago because Cecelia became ill and broke down shortly before she died, telling Rita the entire sordid tale. Jeremy died not knowing he'd fathered a half breed, may he rot."

"I didn't know Rita's mom had passed away," I said sadly, "nor your grandfather."

"Rita is a very private person. Mom just found out Dad and Rita are related when I did. They'd kept it from us until Dad could track down some proof. Apparently, Cecelia had it registered with the Witch Council to protect Rita from future issues. My Great-Aunt Olivia verified the claim and kept it quiet per Cecelia's wishes. None of us knew...but it's legit. My grandfather was not a nice man."

"I'm so sorry, Jake. And I'm sorry I doubted Dennis. He'd been so protective of Rita...now I know why."

"I won't mention the fact you never came to me with any of your suspicions," said Jake wryly. "Let's not make this common knowledge just yet. I'm sure Rita and Dad will in their own time."

"So that means you and Brian are half-cousins!" I cried.

"Yes."

"Does he know?" I asked.

"Not yet. Again...Rita and Dad have been pretty tight-lipped about the entire thing," said Jake.

"I will certainly keep this under wraps. But what is troubling your mom...the voices...now I find out it is happening to my dad as well. And others? How many people are suffering from this malady? And why didn't my parents tell me?" I lamented.

"That is something you are going to have to ask them, Lily," replied Jake.

And ask them I will.

CHAPTER 4

*M*arching with purpose, I wondered once again why I insisted on walking everywhere when I had a perfectly acceptable Jeep to drive. Probably because, in my heightened state of ire, I'd more than likely run over innocent and unsuspecting pedestrians who happened across my path. Now I had to take the time to walk back home to get said Jeep because I needed to have some words with Adriana. Obviously, she knew about my father. The nervous banter between her and Susanne made sense now.

Yesterday afternoon when they'd shown up, neither of them mentioned Charlie, my dad, having similar woes. Oh, it was hinted with their "others" talk, but Adriana decided she'd wait to tell me until the Dennis and Rita issue had been cleared up. Perhaps I would keep their news to myself as punishment. Adriana owed me answers. Nothing and no one would get in the way once I reached my Jeep and was seated behind her trusty wheel.

Well, that would have been the case had I not inadvertently glanced toward June's Emporium and the unlikely figure of a bereft Maureen Kennedy slumped and sobbing on the front stoop.

Now what?

I didn't have time for this. I resolutely turned away and continued my trek toward home. But then curiosity got the better of me—I took a peek in her direction. Oh great. Now Maureen caught me spying on her and...beckoned me over?

I glanced over my shoulder but found myself alone on the sidewalk. Maureen Kennedy wanted to speak to me? The nasty brat who was the bane of teenaged and young adults the town over? She and I had never seen eye to eye; as a matter of fact, the girl was downright surly with me and had a sour disposition that left me with minimal sympathy to spare.

"Are you OK?"

Fine. I could ask, at least. I was the mature one here.

Sometimes.

"Do I look OK?" Maureen sniffed.

Grr. This child tried my patience on a good day. I wasn't about to allow her to level the snark at me and take it when I had pressing issues waiting for my attention. I made to spin around and be on my way when Maureen instantly became contrite.

"I'm sorry. Wait. I..."

Whoa. Did she actually apologize? Worlds must be colliding.

I took in her appearance, and despite the ugly tears, it seems the spiteful young adult had shed pounds, attended to her hair and nails, and tried to groom herself for once. Could she finally be maturing, leaving the pathetic shrew behind?

"What's going on?" I asked.

"I need your help," Maureen meekly admitted. "I'm hearing voices."

Her too? What was going on around here?

"Maybe you are overtired? Or..."

"It's not just that, Ms. Sweet. My magic...it's...it's wonky!"

Wonky? As in my kind of spell going awry wonky? Maureen had my full attention.

"It's just the simplest of spells too. Nothing major...not that I'm a witch with the caliber of spells like your family," she said glumly. "But what little spellcasting I can perform has suddenly gone wacky. I can't even light a candle!"

I felt her. I really did. The first time I tried that little trick, I'd almost burned down my kitchen. Heck, I had dishrags on weekly order for a time until I got the hang of it. Dark magic? The tough stuff? Somehow I knew how to perform a spell with stellar results without honestly knowing what I was doing. The regular old mundane everyday stuff? I had Shirley Jones, our local EMT, on standby—her number on the top of my list to be speed dialed whenever I attempted something trivial.

Yeah, it was that bad.

"I figured, what with *your* history..."

I bit back a nasty retort and tried to put myself in Maureen's shoes.

"Did the wonky magic start at the same time the voices did? And what are these voices like? Is it one? Many?" I asked.

"I'm not sure. Sometimes I'm convinced it is someone I know but can't place...other times, it sounds like many of them whispering nonsense. And yes...within a few days of the voices in my head, my magic went plum wrong. It's been like this for two weeks now."

I briefly wondered if this was happening to everyone suffering this mysterious malady or if Maureen had the novelty of being the only one affected.

"What can I do?" I asked.

Looking at me with haunted eyes, Maureen's lower lip

began to tremble once more.

"I know you're powerful. Your whole blasted family is. You don't have to help me if you don't want to. It's just...I'm so exhausted."

I could see the verity behind her words. Maureen looked awful.

"You know what? Just forget it. You people think you're better than everyone else. You are a pathetic excuse for a witch anyway," she screamed.

Whoa! Hang on now!

"Maureen. What is your problem? Forget I asked that because I know. I know about your family situation. I know a bit of what you have gone through..."

"You know nothing! How could you? Miss Perfect Bitch!"

I was about to turn on my heel but stopped. I had to force myself to keep from reacting negatively. Seeing as this conversation was devolving into something from which we might never be able to return, I chose my subsequent words carefully.

"Maureen, you are a bully."

Well, maybe I didn't feel like treading on thin ice with caution. Sue me.

I barreled ahead.

"Do you know the famous quote? 'All cruelty springs from weakness?' No? I have often thought most bullies are so hurt inside and devoid of love—or a certain type of love they feel they should have received—that they lash out at anyone they perceive to be weaker. They bully to inflict hurt on another so they can feel good about themselves."

"Whatever."

"No. Not whatever, Maureen. I know how much you probably look up to your father. But the man purportedly has demons he is dealing with. The lack of attention, the cruelty he inflicts on your mother, you...your siblings. That kind of hurt can have far-reaching ramifications. In all your years terrorizing the youth in this town, you never considered the pain you caused festering in the minds of those at the receiving end of your caustic tongue."

"Who cares what they think?" barked Maureen, red splotches marring her face.

"You should. We're witches. We know what positive energy and negative energy can do. Think of all those kids you picked on growing up and heading out into the world, finally away from your particular kind of vitriol. These young adults flourish. They move on and grow. But every once in a while, something causes their thoughts to return to their school days and you. And they send negative judgments your way. All those you've hurt, that energy will be directed at you even if you have no idea it's coming. What do you think that does?"

"I'm a strong enough witch. I can burn a black candle. Smudge," she sniffed.

"Are you through? Truly? Then why are you working part time for June for slightly better than minimum wage? June sees something in you, Maureen. Although I have no idea what that could be. But imagine if you will, had you taken your pain, disappointment, and hurt, and instead of castigating more gentle souls, you offer a kind word or deed. What if you were someone who sent out positive energy instead of that tormentor energy? Now think of the same people having pleasant reverie of their time with you in school and beyond. Think of all that positive energy coming to you instead. Don't you think your life might be a tad better without constantly warding off the negative energy?"

I watched Maureen's face crumble, and she began to sob anew.

"It's too late for me. Just leave me alone."

I took pity on her, placing my hand on her shoulder.

"I'm just finding out about these voices afflicting some townsfolk. Unfortunately, you aren't the only one suffering from this. I will see what I can do. For you as well."

The relief in her eyes gave me pause. I could see gratitude and a bit of wonder. As if my generosity was unexpected...and in a way, Maureen might be correct to mistrust me. I let her have it on occasion as good as she doled out. However, I wouldn't stand by and watch anyone become a victim of an unknown evil.

"Th...thank you," she whispered.

Well, that was something, at least. Perhaps there was hope, even for Maureen.

Whatever or whoever was behind these voices had to be deranged. Who would want to cause this much stress to so many? I wondered if my dad, Dennis, and Maureen were the only ones aggrieved or if more and more townsfolk would step forward and admit they were under attack?

"I'm on it," I sighed. Didn't I just say this to Adriana and Susanne?

* * *

I'D JUST REACHED my back porch when I heard them.

Actually, their smell hit me way before I heard the panting, then spied the horrors awaiting me on the back steps.

"Oh no. No way. Not again."

Wondering how the wood could hold up under the combined weight of the two dark purple monstrosities reclining on them, I expected to hear cracking. Instead, their bloodred eyes tracked my every movement while yellow dagger-like teeth glistened in the late afternoon sun. I was amazed when the floorboards didn't sag. Tongues lolling about their massive jaws, I noted in dismay the foul stench was still all-encompassing when it came to these two.

Hellhounds!

Sitting behind the two brutes was none other than my often absent, habitually late friend, Pandora.

"Dorie! Why are you with these monsters? What are the hellhounds doing here exactly?"

"Come say hi, Lily. Max and Rex miss you so."

"Miss me? I hardly think...gah!"

The two unwieldy brutes barreled at me en masse, hitting me with their slobber and stink, until the momentum propelled the three of us backward, and I landed on my back. Rex and Max blocked the setting sun with the magnitude of their form. It was like falling down one mountain only to roll to the base of another. No light could hope to reach the foundation of such lofty, immense muscle and bone. Drool began raining down on me with abandon.

I may have vomited a little in my mouth.

"Help?"

"Woman! Stop goofing off and get up here. We have lots to discuss," chided Dorie.

Seriously? Did she think I'd partake in this embarrassing display of doggy affection willingly?

I only had one eye left with which to peer up at the cross-roads demon, my other having suffered from a direct hit of hellhound slobber, and I found her impatiently tapping one sneaker, hands on hips.

Wait a minute! Pandora...in flats?

The seriousness of the situation just hit home if the impish fashionista was bedecked in everyday loafers!

"How come you have the dynamic duo demon dogs? And why do I think you've come bearing bad news?"

"Oh, it's worse than bad. It's life-altering, Lily. Now get inside where we can have some privacy."

My day went from bad, to worse, to *why did I get up this morning anyway?*

CHAPTER 5

"What is so dire you'd come all the way back from wherever you were hanging with Maggie and Ellie?" I asked.

"New Orleans is overrated. Too many drunk youngsters flashing their boobs or throwing up and passing out on the sidewalk," Dorie sniffed. "The food is great. And the voodoo is always a lively diversion, however."

"Then why did you leave?"

"I won't stay long unless you need me to. I came back at the bequest of Adelaide, and I'm not sure I know what to do for Charlie," said Dorie.

"My mom called you? Is it about the voices he's hearing?" I asked, perturbed I'd been left out of the loop. Again.

"Yes, and don't get that look, Lily. It's written all over your face. You're butt hurt your folks didn't confide in you first," Pandora chided me.

First? How about at all?

"I'm not butt hurt!" I cried.

"You're so butt hurt I'm surprised you can sit for so long without squirming."

Pandora elevated her brows, showing disbelief at my protestations even as she glanced at my non-squirming bottom.

"Explain then," I said. "What exactly is going on?"

"That's just it, Lily. I can't find anything wrong with Charlie." Dorie slumped in her chair and rested her chin in her hands. "I scanned his memory, searched for signs of tampering, and even hit him with a divination spell to see if any residual magic was present from a hostile source. Nothing!"

"I don't understand, Dorie. How can you tell if someone hears voices?" I asked. "I mean, you don't think he's making it up, do you? Because Jake informed me his dad has been having the same issues. Adriana showed up this afternoon and practically ordered me to find out what's going on with him," I stated grumpily, remembering the impolite way she'd disturbed Lorcan's and my nap.

"I can't tell if someone hears voices. I can only discern if they are coming via a spell or incantation," Dorie replied.

"But you said you scanned his memory..."

"That was to see if he was lying."

"Pandora! How could you..."

"Stop, Lily." Dorie held up her hand to stave off any tirade forthcoming. "You know as well as I, Charlie has been through decades of horrific manipulation and tinted magic. Something like that can do a number on anyone. I had to ensure he wasn't suffering from flashbacks or PTSD-type influence."

"Why didn't my mom call me? Am I that horrible a witch she couldn't turn to me in a time of need?" I asked in a quiet voice.

"Lily Sweet! Do *not* go there. Not a pity party. Not from you!" cried Dorie.

I threw my hands in the air, stood, and began to pace a

path from my den to the kitchen and back. Wicked, lazing away the evening on the back of the armchair closest to the fireplace, lifted her head briefly but decided it wasn't worth disturbing her nap over. She placed her head back down onto her front paws and went back to sleep.

Max and Rex became alarmed at my ranting and stomping. Then, sensing my distress, began to howl on my back porch.

"And just why are those two brutes here anyway? It's not like I can keep them, Dorie. What will the neighbors think?" I cried. "Max and Rex are the sizes of a small rhinoceroses. What am I supposed to tell them?"

"What neighbors? The Fergusons moved away..."

"Jorgensons."

"Whatever. They moved away, and their house next door is empty. The house on your other side belonged to that Peterson fella who moved down to Florida to be with his daughter and is so thoroughly covered in kudzu, no one will ever buy the thing."

"Mr. Peterson?" I joked.

"Ha, ha. The house," replied Dorie.

"The Peterson house is not covered in kudzu vines, Pandora. Only the shed is."

"For now," she sniffed. Dorie wasn't her usual jocular and teasing self. Instead, she seemed pensive and subdued, and that alone worried me.

"Dorie, what's up? You seem more upset about this than some other issues that crossed our path. Those you tackled head-on with humor and alacrity. But this new you, it scares me a little."

Pandora leaned back in her seat and then stretched, raising her arms well above her head. She let out a great, big whoosh of air and regarded me dourly. "You want me to joke about half the town hearing voices and running off into the night when the rest of us don't hear a thing and can't find any reason for their behavior? Lily, where have you been? This town is falling apart at the seams! Heck, the autumn tourist season starts in five days. Tanaquil and Olivia are making noises about canceling Opening Day!"

What?

"I've been locked away in my warehouse preparing for just that. I have orders for my new witchy whirligigs and motion art, and I'm working nonstop to prepare my booth for next week. The last thing I want is to run out of supplies or items to sell...so several times in the last few days, I drove down to Atlanta to get more stuff. Plus, now that I'm on the Council, postponing Opening Day would have to be run by me!"

I didn't like having to defend myself or my actions. I worked hard over three weeks on my art, looking forward to the Fall Festival—until now, that is.

"OK, calm down. I didn't mean anything by it. I'm stressed," said Dorie. "I get grumpy when stressed." Pandora reached for an open bag of salted and roasted peanuts and shoved a few in her mouth.

"Just how many people are we talking about here?" I asked.

"Well, apparently, it all started months ago with Shirley," said Dorie, quickly munching and then swallowing before responding.

"Shirley? Shirley Jones, our EMT tech?"

Pandora nodded. And here I thought the odd behavior Shirley had exhibited the past summer had been due to her encounter with that Alan guy who was hired by crazy Deanna Fredricks to kidnap some of my friends and family. But upon further reflection, Shirley stated her mind had been mucked with, her memories tainted. Alan was a human and couldn't have done such a thing. And Deanna hadn't made her presence known yet. So, who or what stole Shirley's memory? And did this have anything to do with the voices she'd heard?

I motioned for Pandora to continue. But instead, she pulled out her cell phone and began scrolling through some kind of a list.

"Charlie was the next to hear voices, although for months he'd not confided a thing to anyone. Not even your mother. Then we have Dennis Carter, Chester Soule, Hermione Winters, Dev Patel, Cornelius Dietrich, Jack Borza, Phillipe LaBlanc, Julia Crawley, Valerie Parks, Lowell Hickinbottom, and Rusty Gooch."

"Add Maureen Kennedy to the mix. She just informed me she too is hearing strange voices in the night," I said.

Pandora shook her head and added Maureen's name to her phone notepad.

I recognized most of those names, but a few were a mystery. Jack was the young apprentice mechanic that worked for Lorcan, and I assumed he hadn't shared his voice-hearing woes with my fiancé.

"Who is Phillipe LaBlanc?" I asked.

"The owner of Phillipe's French Café. You know...that darling place we got my escargot a few months back?"

Ah...yes. The Saveurs brand of snail. *Blech!*

"Why does the name Julia Crawley sound familiar?" I asked.

"Dead guy. Owen. When Antonio gets sucked into the prison? She's his aunt?" Dorie reminded me.

Jeebers! I'd just thought of Owen as a potential beau of Edith's. But, unfortunately, Julia is his aunt and not a fan of me...or my family. Plus, she's an ally of Wilhelmina—and we all know how much that woman hates us!

I continued with my queries. "Who is Valerie Parks? I've never heard that name."

"She's the new assistant vet over at Doc Holcomb's practice," explained Dorie.

I didn't know Doc Holcomb had a new assistant. With that mystery solved, only two names remained.

"Lowell Hickinbottom? That's an unusual name. Who's he?"

"Lily! Seriously? Have you no shame? You say hello to the man every time you work your *Found Things* booth at the fairgrounds!" cried Dorie, slapping her hand down on the table and causing the peanuts to scatter.

I do?

"He's the groundskeeper and nightwatchman."

"Oh! Yes! I do know him. I just never caught his name. When does the man sleep? He's there all day and works the night shift?" I asked, puzzled at the long hours the man must work.

"He's a cryptwalker, silly."

"A crypt what?"

"It's kind of like a graveyard worker. Only it's a Breed. Cryptwalkers don't need much sleep, if any. I mean, they *are* half dead."

"Oh, well...wait, what?"

Sweat trickled down my face, and I instantly felt goosebumps tickle my skin.

"Relax. Lowell's harmless. Well, unless you're dead or a paranormal who got buried alive or something. Then, he'll sniff out those who don't belong in one of his graves and dig you up. Kind of handy—especially for vampires who may have gotten staked and buried alive. Ha! Alive...vampires. Get it?" snorted Dorie. "Lowell works at all the local cemeteries as a gravedigger. It's obviously handy because if someone is stuck underground, before long, Lowell will find them."

How nice.

I chose to move on because I was exhausted by this point,

and one more fantastical bit of information coming at me would cause irreparable brain damage. Half dead Breed? Yeah, no thanks.

"And Rusty Gooch?"

"How could you forget Rusty? Frank's dog?"

"Rusty Gooch is Old Frank's *dog*? You mean...he who ate the prison key, Rusty? Why does he have the last name Gooch?"

"Because it's Frank's last name, silly!" replied Dorie with a giggle.

Frank and Abner, his brother and my caretaker, had the last name Gooch? So that meant Old Greg was a Gooch as well. How had I not known this?

"Hang on a minute. How the heck can a dog hear voices? What I mean is, how could anyone recognize he's hearing them? He's a dog!" I asked in frustration. My head was throbbing. That irreparable damage to my brain was already causing a tic on the left side of my face.

"He wakes up in the dead of night and runs off in the woods, howling. Been doin' it every night for three weeks straight. Rusty...not Frank. Scared Frank right out of his boots, he did."

Gah!

"Abner! You scared me out of my...well, *not* boots, I'm not wearing any. Where did you come from?"

My stealthy handyman had the dreadful habit of sneaking up and startling me with regularity. You'd think I'd be used to it by now.

I'm not.

"Regarding Frank, I assume you don't mean literally—boots. I'm sure Frank doesn't sleep in them," I stated.

"If you say so." Abner seemed confused at my proclamation, confounding him, like I'd said something outlandish and not the other way around. But, despite that, I was confi-

37

dent Old Frank managed to remove those boots at night before climbing into bed.

Surely he must!

Shaking my head to clear it of my reverie, I got back to the matter at hand.

"But why does Frank suspect voices? I mean, sure...I can understand the townsfolk being affected. Why Rusty? Can't he have heard a deer or other critter and gone off barking and chasing that into the woods?"

Abner scratched his head, giving me another weighted look. Ignoring the pity I spied there, I kept a bland, slightly mental smile plastered to my face.

I was hoping I came across as wise and agreeable.

"If you say so...but that's not what's happening. Rusty can be doing something normal like herding the chickens or eating his supper when up goes his head, quick like, and he looks around. Then he bays and runs off. Sometimes he is asleep next to Frank, then pops up and barks to be let out, then runs off, not returning until morning. It's not normal night noises...at least that's what he told Frank."

Oh, well then...wait! No. Just...no.

I refuse to consider a talking dog. My cat was enough, thank you. I didn't need a magical talking dog to ruin the rest of an unpleasant day.

"Mebbe you should ask him yourself?" said Abner.

And there you go. Day. Ruined.

I would never consider trying to communicate with Rusty except for saying "fetch" or "sit."

I sat back down and rested my forehead on the table, refusing to engage any further until my headache subsided.

I was toast.

CHAPTER 6

"What's with her?"

I heard my great-grandmother enter the kitchen and swish over to the table where I'd remained head down, in shock for the better part of an hour now. Pandora had offered Abner a soda and some snacks, and he'd accepted. The two of them were on their second cola in the time I'd remained prone.

"Oh, Lily is just being dramatic," said Dorie.

I raised my head and glared at no one in particular.

"Why is there a peanut on your forehead, Lily. Must you play games?" sniffed Adriana. Reaching up, she plucked the offending legume off my face and popped it in her mouth.

I opened mine wide to make a comment, but my jaw remained unhinged—stuck open in utter amazement. Finally, I managed to slam it and my unbelieving eyes shut. Still, when I peeked out at Adriana, the visage she'd chosen to show the world today hadn't altered.

"What on earth are you wearing?" I stuttered out.

I belatedly noticed Susanne, assuming she'd arrived with

Adriana, and nodded hello but kept my eyes fastened to that garish guise.

"This old thing? I decided I needed a new summer sleuthing outfit and pulled this beauty out of my trunk."

"The one that should have gone to Goodwill in the 1960s?" I asked in disbelief.

Susanne snorted.

Adriana, for all intents and purposes, looked like some kind of aging stripper from long ago. Back when props and burlesque moves trumped the gyrating pole-dancing athletics of today.

Her outfit, chartreuse green, turquoise, and brown, was made of scarves. I was positive she could yank them out at will and whirl them around her head in some kind of seductive dance—this alone made me shudder.

That and the fact one could easily tell Adriana had skipped wearing a bra.

Adriana's ensemble came complete with sandals on her feet—tiny shells and bells sewn along the seam chimed a dainty little tune with every step. A headband that matched graced her noggin. She'd even let down her lengthy hair which reached her lower back in a cascade of grey and black.

"Gypsy Rose Lee called. She wants her outfit back," I snarked.

"Hardy har, har. Gypsy was more the sequins and feather boa type. I will have you know this belonged to the late, great Lenore LaRue. She used to knock 'em dead at her show in Paris," said Adriana, lifting her hands with a flourish.

"France?" asked Dorie, her enthusiasm for the city apparent.

"Texas," replied Adriana.

OK, then.

Abner smiled and did a little dance—either that or he had gas.

"You could give anyone a show, Miz Dolce. You'd pack the house for sure," he gushed. But, of course, this went straight to my grandmother's head, and she beamed at him.

"You know, I could at that!"

"Yes...well. Before you start the *Dance of the Seven Veils*, you better explain to me why you are here and what you want. Then you can tell me why my family, you included, decided to *not* inform me of my dad's current condition," I grumped. "Or the fact the rest of the town has the same affliction."

"You didn't ask?"

"Try again."

"We forgot?"

I crossed my arms and began to tap my foot on the wood floor.

"We assumed you knew?" Adriana looked wary and wouldn't meet my eyes.

"What's worse is my dad didn't trust me enough to say anything," I wailed.

"Did you remotely consider we may have wanted to spare you this latest bit of news since you've had so much on your plate as of late?" Adriana asked airily. "Not to mention you've been buried in wedding plans. Maybe we wanted to free you from such concerns."

I paused, eyes widening, my heart swelling with fuzzy feelings. My emotions were instantly hijacked with thoughts of my family thinking only the best of intentions where I was concerned.

Yeah. It didn't last. While I was confident of my family's love for me, the way everyone kept secrets and left me in the dark, you'd think I was a mushroom or something. I came crashing down to reality rather quickly.

"Nice try. Now, what are you really doing here?"

Adriana scowled. "Word on the street is you're investigating the strange voices."

Word on the...?

"Just how efficient is the Gossip Gang? All I did was visit with Jake as you and Susanne suggested. No further investigation was forthcoming. And why did you send me on a fact-finding mission when you knew all along it was about voices —and not extramarital affairs?"

"I didn't! I had to be certain this wasn't some kind of lover's spat with Rita using her dark magic to cause some mischief that spread from Dennis to the rest of the town," said Adriana. "The last thing I want is more aspersions touching our kind."

By our kind, I assumed dark witches.

"But why me? You couldn't make a surprise visit to Rita and just ask?"

"I may have recently pissed her off, and now we aren't on speaking terms."

Why doesn't this surprise me?

"What did you do?" I asked in consternation.

"I may have accused her of using cheap essential oils in her shop, trying to cut corners, instead of the top-of-the-line products she used to carry. She denies it, of course. Asked me to leave, and we haven't spoken since."

Great.

"Do you suspect Rita has been in cahoots with our enemies? I know Rowan Nightingale's family was close to her. Still, after we ended that fiasco, nary a word of Rita being involved was ever voiced," I stated. "Right?"

"June's been guarded. Enough so Petunia noticed and started this current chin-wagging. I asked her last week what had upset her so, but she insisted it was these voices Dennis had been hearing. Yet she seems preoccupied with Rita—and I want to know why!" Adriana slammed her fist in the opposite hand. I watched as she began to pace, her scarves creating a floating trail with every pass.

Yep, no underwear, either.

Susanne jumped in. "Petunia keeps showing up at the Emporium purportedly for one item or another but never buying much. She keeps dropping Rita's name with her forked tongue—the viper. Poor June gets so flummoxed every time. It sent up quite the red flag. Why...she was even there yesterday before we came to see you. Petunia couldn't resist her speculating, and the Gossip Gang was off and running."

I sat back with a smug smile on my face. A perfect image of the cat that ate the canary. I finally knew something that no one else did—except for Jake, et al.

I relished in the knowledge that I had a bit of gossip to share.

Then I sobered. My grin slipped as the realization hit I couldn't share what I'd learned with anyone yet. So I quickly tried to figure out a ruse to explain the Dennis and Rita situation without giving away their secret.

Blast and darn!

"What's up, Lily? Your face just ran the gamut of emotions, and now you look guilty as hell. And that's a place I'm familiar with," said Pandora wryly.

"Um...I was just thinking how upsetting this must be for June. And...Dennis...Rita..."

"What did you learn?" barked Adriana like a hound on the scent of its prey.

"I can't tell you yet."

"Don't you dare get all snippy just because we didn't tell you about the voices," she cried.

"I'm not! I just can't say anything yet," I protested.

Adriana squinted, and even Susanne seemed a bit

perturbed. Dorie was about to say something when Edith popped in.

"You'll never believe what I learned about Rita and Dennis!" she cried.

"Wait! Edith...no..."

"I heard from a trusted source that Rita and Dennis have a love child they gave up for adoption, and now that person has contacted June, causing all manner of woe."

I snapped my mouth shut and let it go. Perhaps everyone would buy that little tale, and I'd be off the hook.

"Really? Well, I can certainly see why June would be upset. However, we shouldn't bring it up unless she reaches out to us first," Susanne said.

And just like that, my worries were over.

That is until I caught Dorie staring at me knowingly. I knew she'd corner me when we were alone and force me to spill the beans.

Little did she know my tenacity knew no bounds.

CHAPTER 7

*a*fter another half hour of going back and forth with Adriana explaining that I was more than capable of investigating the voices on my own, I finally managed to extract myself from the debate of having to take her with me. Despite her protests to the contrary and the fact she'd dressed for the occasion, I could sense a weariness about her. I reminded Adriana she still had weeks to go before the clerics deemed her fit as a fiddle.

Somehow, Susanne convinced my grandmother to leave me alone. My gratitude was apparent as a protesting Adriana stormed from my house with Susanne and Abner hot on her heels.

That still left a smirking Pandora behind.

"I'm going with you," she stated.

"I'd expect no less."

"I'm going too!" cried Edith. "After all, my quick thinking got you out of spilling the beans about..."

"Edith!"

Glancing in Dorie's direction, my telltale ghost slapped a

hand across her mouth and popped out of existence, leaving a wispy trail of ectoplasm in her wake.

"Spill it, or I'm getting out the thumb screws."

So, I did. On the way to my first stop, I told Dorie everything I'd discussed with Jake and swore her to secrecy. Was I proud of myself for breaking his confidence? No. Did I believe, with everything fiber of my being, that Dorie would torture me as promised to get the information?

You betcha.

I looked at it as self-preservation and hoped Jake would understand.

It would all come out eventually. Because nothing remained a secret for long in Sweet Briar, Georgia.

Now we were riding in my Jeep, Wicked between us, heading to Doc Holcomb's practice to kill two birds with one stone, so to speak. Dev Patel and the new assistant vet, Valerie Parks, worked in his establishment, so why not drop in and get a description of these voices?

Dorie wanted to take Max and Rex so they could be examined and deemed healthy, but firstly, how would I get the two monstrously large behemoths into my Jeep? And second, how does one explain having two hellhounds as pets to the general populace? This would take some finagling, and I thought it best to leave it to Doc Holcomb to devise a way to give both dogs an annual checkup.

"Why did I get saddled with Max and Rex again?" I asked Pandora.

"Who else will take them?" she replied.

"What? What do you mean? I thought they belonged to Frank?" I asked.

"They just stayed there for a bit."

"No. No way. Adriana said they were Frank's and..."

"And I conjured them out of hell for our use," said Pandora with a grin.

"Well, send them back then. I can't keep them! There is no way to explain their existence to Breed, let alone humans. How on earth will I get away with normal doggy duties, like vet visits and romping through the park?"

The last time the beasts were loose at the fairgrounds, they caused a commotion—widespread panic everywhere. Definitely not good for business—mine or anyone else's.

"If I send them back, they will be eliminated, Lily."

"But why?" I was horrified. I might not want to keep Max and Rex, but eliminated? That sounded rather final. "I don't understand."

Pandora sighed and looked out the window at the passing terrain. "I didn't exactly have permission to conjure them."

"And the answer is to...um...do away with them?" I asked.

Dorie didn't answer me right away, instead choosing to continue her survey out the window. She squirmed a few times, and I wondered at her discomfort.

"OK, listen. Even back when I was imprisoned in book form, I could still enter the demon realm. As one myself, I was never hindered from that dimension since the laws are different over there." Dorie scratched her nose and began gnawing on the skin around her thumb.

"Because I was tricked into imprisonment, I was sort of punished on my home turf, if you will, and stuck on what you'd call 'desk duty.' So, while toiling away in mindless boredom, I sort of created Max and Rex as a diversion to keep me company. They were the cutest little puppies, no bigger than a pony, and they kept me sane in an awful situation."

"I don't understand. Why was it so horrible if you were free to visit your realm?" I asked.

"Lily, I was locked away in a cubicle. No windows. No interaction. Shunned and isolated like a failure. Creating the hounds was not the smartest thing I did, but I was going insane being sequestered. Plus, they had me doing the worst kinds of tasks imaginable, and frequently it was easier to just remain stuck as a book."

I couldn't imagine what could be so bad Dorie would choose to while away the years as a book.

"What did they make you do?" I asked in trepidation.

"I had to keep files on all the politicians, lawyers, and evangelical preachers sent south the second they carked it."

Carked? Oh...carcass. *Ew.*

Mother of all things holy! Dorie didn't have to say another word as far as I was concerned, but she continued anyway.

"Do you know how long it takes to process those folks? And the way they'd carry on! You'd think they would have known where they were heading. It still didn't stop them from trying to plead their case—it took me ten times longer to be rid of them than the other souls."

Pandora finally adjusted herself, so she faced me.

"I brought Max and Rex over when I discovered you needed great scent hounds, then gave them to Adriana, who placed them temporarily with Frank. Unfortunately, the hounds will be eliminated because they weren't approved. They are only safe here on this plane."

"But Frank. Can't he...why should I...how can I..."

"Rusty and the other dogs are intimidated. They've been fine as much as canines can be around demon dogs, but Frank said his pack is off their feed, and he's afraid they might get sick as a result. It isn't easy for normal dogs to be around hellhounds. At least, that's what he's claiming. Frank has been acting more strangely than usual. I assume it is due to the stress of dealing with the voices plaguing Rusty. So, you need to take them."

"But I can't! I don't know how I can manage them!"

Pandora looked crestfallen, and I felt like a heel. However,

I didn't waver because I knew I was in the right. There was no way the hellhounds would remain unnoticed in my care. There had to be another way.

"Wait a minute! What about Mortimer? Maybe he can keep them since he tends to live in remote spots. Or...hey now! My fairy godfather, Jerry, might want guard dogs. He constantly complains about looky-loos popping into The Forbidden Library. Maybe he could take them."

Pandora looked hopeful, and I whipped out my phone to call Jerry, hoping to find him on duty and willing to become the proud owner of two demon dogs.

* * *

"WE CAN SET up a visit at the library when Jerry takes possession of Max and Rex," I told Doc Holcomb, who seemed somewhat alarmed he'd be examining my fairy godfather's new pets.

Yes, Jerry came through in a big way. He was overjoyed with the prospect of having two humongous guard dogs keeping pesky busybodies away from his prized—and most dangerous—books. Unfortunately, Jerry just needed some time to prepare for them, so for the time being, I was stuck babysitting.

"Well, I will be glad to examine them both. I assume the hounds are well behaved. I wouldn't want to lose an arm or anything," Doc laughed nervously.

"Do you eat raw meat?" asked Dorie.

"Er...no," replied Doc Holcomb.

"How about cologne? Do you wear anything that smells like rancid flesh?" continued Dorie.

"Definitely not!"

"What about politics?" she asked

"What about them?"

"Do you have an opinion on whether or not I employ one or both dogs to go on political hunts?" Dorie leaned forward, awaiting the veterinarian's response.

"You can do with them whatever you wish. I mean...technically, they are your dogs, I guess. I have no objections as long as they won't come to harm," he replied.

"Oh, it won't be they who come to harm. I assure you," simpered Dorie, leaning back in satisfaction. "You're good. The hounds will love you."

Doc Holcomb darted his eyes in my direction, widening them when they landed on Wicked, who'd followed us in despite my attempts at keeping her in my Jeep. Even if I locked her in, she'd just do her feline magic and follow us anyway.

"Well, that's fine, then," he said, throwing a worried glance in my direction.

I just shrugged my shoulders in a "what can you do?" sort of way.

"Well, that's settled then. What can I do for you ladies today?" asked Doc.

"We need to speak to your new assistant. Valerie, is it? And Dev if he's available. Official Council business," said Dorie.

I frowned and motioned for her to stop, but she ignored me and continued, "We can use your back office for interrogations. Oopsie! I mean, interviews." Dorie giggled and indicated we should precede her to the back room in question.

Oh dear. If word got out about this, I would be in deep doo...member of the Council—and a newly appointed Elder —or not.

"They aren't in any trouble. I mean, Valerie hasn't been here but a few months. And Dev Patel is a paragon in the community," Doc offered.

"This is nothing to fret over," said Dorie. "All they need is to answer our questions honestly, and we'll be on our way."

Great. Pandora talking like a police officer was going to get both of us in trouble for impersonation. Or misrepresentation. Something would go wrong. I just knew it.

This was proven when an irate and highly suspicious Valerie Parks walked into the back room where we'd taken a seat.

"Why are you pretending to be here representing the Council when I know they are unaware of what ails me? My aunt assured me she and Tanaquil were the only ones aware of my condition."

"Who's your aunt?" I asked.

Surely it couldn't be Olivia Ogden-Meyers. That would mean Valerie was related to Brian Chase. I was the one who had relatives dropping out of the eaves. I didn't need the competition from Brian, despite him not knowing about Jake's family and his mother's role in it.

"Gloria Stillwell."

I didn't see that coming. I didn't know Gloria had any kin in the area. She'd often joined my family for gatherings and holidays, so I assumed incorrectly that she had no one close by.

"My mother and Gloria are sisters."

Well, then that explains...nothing. Why didn't Gloria spend time with her kin? Did they live far apart? I'm sure I'd eventually have those answers, but right now we had the matter of the mysterious voices to deal with.

"We are looking into these enigmatic voice complaints. Lily is an Elder, so as such, this is Council business," replied Pandora smugly.

"It is rather a hush-hush issue. I'm sure you can imagine how keeping this under wraps is tantamount to not having the residents of Sweet Briar go into a panic," I added lamely.

"Hey, you kinda look familiar...like I've seen you around town but not in this capacity," said Dorie, scrutinizing the woman a bit closer than was necessary or appropriate.

"If you must know, I have a booth at the fairgrounds and read palms for fun," Valerie replied stiffly.

"You tell fortunes?" I asked curiously.

"I read palms. I give séances. I can even read runes. But basically, I tell foolish men and women what they expect to hear, keeping the truth to myself because most people can't handle it," replied Valerie. "I do it for the extra money, not because I give a fig about love matches and happily ever after for silly mortals who are afraid of the truth."

Tell me how you really feel, why don't you?

"We won't keep you long. We just have a few quick questions then we will be out of your hair. I promise," I offered.

"I think you need to call Dev in here as well. His situation is far more prevalent than mine. Might as well kill two birds with one stone," Valerie offered.

See? That's what I thought. Then, hopefully, we'd get some insight into the odd happenstances and could pinpoint a culprit or some mass sickness to blame. Then, maybe this would be over before someone else started hearing voices.

Me. OK? I had enough on my plate!

"That sounds like a plan. Call in Dev."

Finally, we were getting down to some real sleuthing.

CHAPTER 8

"I don't know what else I can offer. I don't hear words. I hear mumbling but feel compelled to follow their call," said Dev Patel glumly. "I haven't had a decent night's sleep in over a month."

"Same."

I turned to Valerie who had just spoken.

"I don't sleep. I barely eat. I wander the streets at night trying to find whoever is calling out to me. And before you ask, no, I cannot tell what they are saying. I just know I need to get up and search for their whereabouts," Valerie informed us.

"They?" asked Dorie. "As in more than one voice?"

"Yes," Dev and Valerie replied in unison.

How odd. One voice had to be disturbing enough. Multiple mumbling agents had to be torturous.

"Can you discern how many are muttering at the same time?" I asked.

"I'd say at least four," replied Dev.

"Seven," Valerie responded emphatically.

OK, then.

"Have you spoken of this to anyone?" I asked delicately, knowing hearing voices could be construed as borderline insane in some circles.

"Only my aunt and Tanaquil," replied Valerie.

"No one," whispered Dev. "Well, except for Valerie here. She recognized the same symptoms I'm displaying that she's also been suffering and broached the subject with me. I'm indebted to her for reaching out. At least I know I'm not alone—and going mad. Not if other folks are suffering so. Oh! And Chester Soule. He gave me a sample draught Hester concocted to help him sleep. Only it doesn't seem to be working for me. I'll keep using it, however, you never know."

"Maybe you could ask Hester for some for me. I'm so sleep-deprived I almost shaved a cat completely when all I was supposed to do was make a small square section to put in an IV," mumbled Valerie.

Eek.

"I want you to know we plan on solving this. We will find out who or what is behind the voices and deal with them," I promised.

"Good luck. I've never experienced anything like this before," said Valerie.

Dev just looked bummed out.

"We're on it," said Dorie. "Don't worry about a thing. This will be as easy as pie. Lily here is the cat's meow as far as her sleuthing abilities."

Speaking of cats, where had Wicked gotten to? Unfortunately, she wasn't in the room with us, and we needed to move on to our next interview.

"What's that noise?" asked Valerie. "It sounds like a velociraptor got loose in a cow pen!"

Oh no. Not again.

After writing Doc Holcomb an open check and waiting

until the estimation came back for the damages, Dorie and I, with a bound Wicked, moved on to our next stop.

No. I will not go into what happened.

There was blood and fur. I'm sure you can paint the perfect picture.

"That wasn't so bad. That beagle only needed ten stiches and the vet tech readily agreed to not press charges if you pay for her reconstructive surgery." Dorie observed.

Where to...um, next?" asked Dorie losing some enthusiasm as she noticed the scowl on my face.

Yes. It *was* that bad. Use your imagination.

Sighing, I turned the Jeep toward the west side of town. "Let's go see my parents. I probably shouldn't put off the inevitable."

"But I've already spoken with them. Your dad doesn't know what's going on. I can't get a proper reading and..."

"And I'm a shadowdancer. Maybe I can sniff the information out of Dad. It's worth a try, anyway."

"He isn't dead, Lily."

"Yeah...but I'm not any normal shadowdancer. I'm a vampire...and a sweet briar witch. Even if I'm an accidental one. Heck, I even have some demon in me, thanks to you. Who knows what I can conjure up?"

"Hopefully, it won't be another pair of hellhounds," she replied.

She can say that again.

* * *

"Lily. Sweetheart. It's good to see you, dear." My mother, Adelaide, was delighted to see me when I dropped by. My parents opted to move into the massive Victorian home belonging to my great-grandparents, leaving the craftsman home I'd renovated for me and eventually Lorcan, as our home.

"What brings you here?"

"You can drop the innocent act. The cats are out of the bag. Well...not Wicked. She's tied up in a sack in the back of my Jeep."

"Pardon?" Mom peered over my shoulder to see if I was jesting.

I was not.

If you listened carefully, you could hear the growls from my Jeep and feel the animosity pouring from it in our direction.

"Why is Wicked locked in your car?"

"Ask the veterinary hospital...and tell Dad I might need a loan from the trust to pay off the damages," I replied.

Mom looked askance in my direction, her hand to her throat.

"Dorie. Good to see you...I think."

"Addy. Don't mind Lily. She's had a rough couple of days," said Dorie with a roll of her eyes. "Hey, do you have anything to eat? I'm starving."

"I'm sure we can manage something. Come into the kitchen. Your father is making sauce."

We followed Adelaide into the kitchen, where my father was indeed making tomato sauce. The room smelled heavenly, and I didn't realize how hungry I was until that precise moment.

"Hello, baby girl. What brings you here?" asked my dad, giving me a side hug.

I'm ashamed to say I subtly began sniffing my own father to discern any untruths...but my shadowdancer radar remained quiet. Finally, I raised my brows at Dorie, and she shrugged as if to say, "we had to try."

Charlie Sweet had been through hell and back, but

somehow, he exuded pure joy. I'm sure it was due to his having my mom back in his life. Their years apart made the time they now had together all the more poignant, and Dad lived every day like it was a gift. And in a way...I guess it was.

"Unfortunately, I am here like a dark cloud hovering over you in an otherwise cloudless sky," I replied.

"Surely not! What could you possibly mean? We love when you visit. I wish you'd do it more often, but I heard you've spent long hours making your art pieces."

"That might be true. But I'm actually here about the voices you hear that badger you."

You could hear the proverbial pin drop; the room had gone so silent. If it wasn't for the bubbling saucepot, I might think I'd gone deaf.

"Ciao, Bellissima. You make hoppy me to see."

Grandpa Antonio shuffled into the room with a beaming smile when he spied me.

"Ah! Signorina Pandora. You come to make-a me sentiti più giovane! Young again, no?"

"Only if you leave Adriana and take me on a whirlwind trip of Europe," laughed Dorie.

The tension left the room, although I noticed the look that passed between my parents. I decided to not push it for now and spent a few minutes visiting my great-grandfather. He looked robust and lively for his age, and now that I knew he'd suffered for decades from a vampire attack that left him less healthy than other witches his age, I always watched for telltale signs he needed to rest. Unfortunately, he'd inadvertently passed the vampirism to me, leaving much to be desired. But I was trying my best to ignore that part of myself.

It hadn't worked out so great for me. Twice my fangs punched out when I least expected. Usually, when I was in rush hour traffic and cursing up a storm. I had zero ideas how to control them from extending when I was irate.

"Here, set the table, and I will get us some coffee. Dorie? Would you like cookies or cake?" asked Adelaide.

"Yes, please!"

My mother chuckled and went to find goodies to sate Pandora's legendary appetite.

"Shall we light the candles?" asked Charlie, pointing to two long, brown tapers on either end of the table.

"Here, let me."

The significant intake of breath was extinguished when I twirled my hand, and the two candles flickered to life. I gave a jaunty little smirk to my doubters and took a seat.

Fine. So, in the past, mundane spells and how to properly cast them had eluded me. With terrible consequences, I might add. But I'd slowly improved to the point I now felt some confidence in my abilities. As for my dark magic? I might have just surpassed Adriana in that department, and I don't think even she would deny it.

Speak of the devil...

"Liliana. Did you just perform magic in my home? How dare you! Quick...someone call the fire department."

"Very funny. You know darn well I've improved. Nothing happened, and the candles are lit," I responded.

"Yes, well...we can only hope. So why are you here?"

"What...you can drop into my place whenever you feel like it, but when I do the same, I'm met with resistance?" I sputtered.

"Of course not. Lily, your grandma, is kidding," said Adelaide.

"Am not..."

"She doesn't mean anything by it," cried Adelaide throwing Adriana an exasperated look.

"I mean what I mean. Lily is a loose cannon and probably will be forever," sniffed Adriana.

"Centuries? Surely I won't live that long," I nervously laughed.

"Why not? You're a part vamp. I expect the world will be stuck with you for a very long time."

I didn't know what to say to that, so I tried to steer the conversation toward the mystery voices.

"I don't know why you're surprised to find me here. You asked me to look into the voices everyone's been hearing. Well, not everyone—some townsfolk."

"I did no such thing!" shouted Adriana.

"You did too! Lower your voice, you loon!"

"Did not!"

"Did too!"

"Did not, you big dummy," cried Adriana.

"You did too, and you brought Susanne. And you tried to get Wicked involved," I cried.

"I asked you to find out the issue between Dennis and Rita. I never once asked you to meddle in things you should stay far away from," replied Adriana.

How dare she!

Here I am, trying to help...at her request, even if she did so in a roundabout way, and now she denies it in front of everyone else? No way, sister!

"I backed you into a corner over the very issue of these voices plaguing half the town, and you're just bent that I left you out of the sleuthing part. I don't need your help, old lady! I can be a detective, smash rumors and gossip and even perform the most basic of magical tasks...why..."

BOOM!

"What are you waiting for? Call the fire department!" Then I just sighed.

CHAPTER 9

"We can take it to the dealership tomorrow. The good news is that it's under warranty."

Lorcan rubbed his hand up and down my back, offering sympathy and taking control of an abysmal situation. Then he heard the sirens, watched the fire truck head out of town toward my great-grandparents' home, and decided it might be prudent to follow.

"Did you really set your Jeep on fire?" asked Andrea.

Of course, she'd returned. Why was it that every time something magical went wonky by my hand, Andrea was there to gawp at the shock and awe of it all?

"It was glorious," barked Dorie. "You should have seen Lily run as fast as a cheetah on acid to save Wicked."

"Wicked was perfectly fine and managed to extinguish the diminutive inferno in a matter of seconds," I explained through gritted teeth.

"With a copious amount of cat urine," chortled Dorie.

I may have motioned to wring her neck, but no one paid me any mind since they were transfixed on my smoking Jeep.

Wicked, in a feat of self-preservation, managed to slip out

of her tether and pounce on the smoldering spot on my front seat. Yes, I managed to set my bucket seat ablaze, even if it was a little fire.

"You got the incantation wrong," cackled Adriana.

"It's OK, honey. You never learned the proper nuance as a child. We didn't do good by you," cried Adelaide, looking morose. "Either that or Latin isn't your strong point."

"*Lux ignis cereus fuscus ubi est* was the proper term. However, your incantation, *lux scintilla cereus fuscus ubi est,* was wrong," Adriana explained. "Basically, you shot a firecracker in the opposite direction from which you lit those tapers."

"I thought scintilla meant ignite!" I wailed.

"No. It means spark, Squirt. Ignis...ignite. Get it? Nice one there, however. I need to remember it for July Fourth."

Adriana had tears running down her face, and I'd not seen her so lively in months. Glad I could be of service.

"The important thing is Lily tried, and she is getting better. She did manage to light the candles on the table," said Charlie, helpfully, putting his arm around me and pulling me close.

Gee, thanks, Dad.

"What are you doing here?" I asked Andrea glumly.

"Mom and Dad are coming over for dinner tonight, and I thought I'd tag along," Andrea replied, sounding hurt at my acerbic attitude.

Andrea's mom, Chiara, and my dad were siblings. Their parents died young in a car crash, leaving them orphaned and raised by their grandparents, Adriana and Antonio. Uncle Stephen, Iona's husband, ran a bakery café and made the most delightful delicacies imaginable.

"Your dad bringing a pastry box?" I asked.

Andrea brightened considerably, "You know it."

Turning to Lorcan and ignoring Adriana's posturing, I

said, "You're done for the day, sweetie. We're staying for dinner. Plus, despite what some people are inferring, I was tasked to get to the bottom of these voices. And I need to speak with everyone who's suffering. That includes you, Dad," I said, addressing Charlie, who looked resigned.

"Let's head back inside," Adelaide said as the tow truck arrived.

Lorcan indicated he'd remain behind to deal with it and then would follow us. I just hoped he'd come up with a reasonable explanation as to why a hole was burned in the center of my seat. That is until I realized the tow truck driver was Stu Jones, Lorcan's mechanic and our esteemed mayor —don't ask.

"Did it again, didn't you?" Stu shouted down at me before I could beat a hasty retreat.

I waved my hand over my head and continued up the porch steps and into the house. And I may have only used one finger for that wave.

* * *

"AND YOU CAN'T MAKE out a thing they say?" I asked my dad.

"Nothing."

Charlie looked uncomfortable answering me but was resigned to do so. We had to get to the bottom of this situation, and since everyone assumed I'd put on my sleuthing cap —and I had—they would finally open up and let me do my job. Why me, and not call in Brian Chase, remained a mystery until Adelaide spoke up.

"Lily, we tried to keep you from finding out about this," she began.

No, really? You think?

"But it's not what you may think. As a new Elder, you need to take on a role in one of the divisions at the Witch

Council, as you well know. So our enemies put in a petition that you be named Head of Oddities and work in The Forbidden Library with Jerry," said Adelaide.

"Gloria Stillwell put a petition to make you Head of Investigations, for the investigative task force, instead. You see...with your natural urge to snoop into things, she thought you might want to be head of that new division at the Witch Council," explained Charlie.

Hang on a minute!

"Why me and not Brian? He's a detective!" I cried. "And what nerve! I know I sport a large target on my back where our enemies are concerned but sitting in The Forbidden Library all day is not my idea of a pleasant task."

"That's what Olivia stated, although she'd rather not have you as Head Investigator either and suggested her nephew. But Brian offered it should be you instead to keep him able to juggle duties on the outside as his position with the state of Georgia allows and is available to us," Adelaide continued.

"But what does that have to do with why you've kept me in the dark?" I asked.

"We, your grandparents, your dad...everyone really. We felt you might not appreciate being looked at as...well..."

"Gloria and everyone involved reasons due to your close proximity to everything bad happening around here as of late, they might as well make you in charge of investigating them in an official capacity—at least the Elders on our side think this. Wilhelmina and her ilk want you locked away, so saddled with paperwork and red tape you wouldn't be able to cause chaos," Adriana explained.

"Basically, they think you are behind the voices, and locking you in a room all day to do research is the safest way of eliminating the threat," Charlie said, looking abashed at having expressed the real reason I'd been selected.

"So, all this time, you were what? Keeping this from me until some kind of vote?"

"No. We've been trying to convince the Elders not to approach you with this. That you had no idea the town was going insane was proof in a way that you had nothing to do with it," explained Adelaide. "At least it backed our enemies off. Even Wilhelmina had to admit you were walking around clueless and, I quote, 'no one could pull off stupid that well.' I'm sorry, dear. We were just trying to keep them from finding a reason to believe you really are behind the voices."

Of all the nerve. Those Dietrich and Langsfords...even the Planks and their cronies. All of them could take a jump off the highest bridge for all I cared. Stupid. I will show them stupid...or, er...not.

"There has to be a reason they thought I had something to do with this. It can't be just because they hate me. What's the real reason?"

Adriana nodded her head in approval at my acumen.

"Indeed. You may not know this, but Judge Dietrich has been afflicted as well," she said.

"Pandora gave me a list of folks, and he was mentioned," I replied. "I knew he was among those suffering."

"As it would seem, the good judge indicated he alone can decipher words among the mumbling. And the voices keep mentioning you by name," declared Adriana. "You can imagine how well that sits with our enemies."

"Me? What are they saying?" I asked, shocked.

"That we do not know," said Adelaide. "But Wilhelmina wants you nowhere near the judge or in a position to question him. Hence making you head of recordkeeping for all things odd. Sequestered away in The Forbidden Library all day, you'd have no time to investigate."

"What does Judge Dietrich say?" I asked, aghast that I might find myself locked in a place I hoped to never return.

Over my dead body...by the way, in case you were wondering!

"Again, we have absolutely no idea—because he's disappeared," said Adelaide.

"Or Wilhelmina has him locked away somewhere," sniffed Adriana. "I told you something evil was afoot in this town. You need to find Cornelius! But you're going to need some answers for this type of magic. And there is only one place you will be able to find them."

Wicked came through loud and clear with no one the wiser. And I instantly knew where she wanted me to find those answers.

Why did I not see this one coming?

CHAPTER 10

hree days had passed, and I was back in my Jeep with Edith riding shotgun. It was evening, and we headed up the highway back toward Sweet Briar. Surprisingly, the dealership had a bucket seat that matched my model ready and waiting, and I was returning from having it installed.

OK. Fine.

I may have suggested to Dewayne Funk, the befuddled young car salesman who'd sold it to me this past February, that he should unbolt one from a matching model and have it installed in my Jeep in record time. And by suggest, I meant magic—I used magic on him. This spread across the repair shop like a coiling wisp of smoke, bewitching everyone it came in contact with so no one questioned a thing.

Dark magic. Gotta love it.

Andrea had graciously offered to drive me down to Clayton, Georgia to pick it up. She now followed behind me in her Subaru Outback. Why Andrea gave up a perfectly awesome old Jeep Laredo was beyond me. Still, she loved her little car, which was probably decent on gas.

We had plans to meet at my place, where she'd parked, and ride in the Jeep with me, Pandora, and Adriana for a bit of nighttime sleuthing. I tried to talk Adriana out of coming along with us, explaining that we would just observe and not do anything nefarious. But I don't think we fooled her one bit.

Where are we going, you ask?

Why...we've decided to finally break into the Dietrich compound and find the judge's whereabouts. The last time we attempted this, we'd witnessed a poor, unfortunate, Heathcliff Fitzwillow, get lit up like a torch and magically burned to a crisp by a bunch of rampaging demons, thanks to that lunatic Tiffany Clarkson. We never made it onto the estate, instead having our own demon battle off in the woods that bordered the property.

I still had the map of the place that Cousin Nora drew for me—yeah, I know, Nora being helpful was quite the shocker. She still hates me, and I'm not a fan, but a truce of sorts is now in effect, and she is living back home with my Aunt Iona and Uncle Owen, much to their delight.

If Judge Dietrich is being held against his will by his kin, or if he is willingly in hiding, I can't think of a better place to do so than the Dietrich/Langsford estate.

It should really be the Langsford and Plank estate, but poor Arthur Plank was overshadowed by his wife, Stella, and her mother, Wilhelmina, just as Boris Langsford deferred to his wife. Wilhelmina was a Dietrich and kept loyal to her clan, so poor Boris didn't make waves. I'm just surprised they gave their daughter, Stella, his surname and didn't force the issue. Therefore, the compound was known locally as the Dietrich/Langsford estate.

Edith loved her family, but even she was finished with their insanity and was now loyal to me. Mother Stella and

Grandmother Wilhelmina made it difficult for forgiveness—their scheming against my family had become ridiculous.

"We're almost home. Do you think Lorcan managed to distract Adriana so we can do this without her coming along?" asked Edith. "And has he found the map yet?"

Nora, a frequent visitor when Edith was alive and well, drew up a map of the areas she'd memorized, and Edith herself finished those places only kin were privy to. As far as we were concerned, there were three main areas of interest on which we would focus—the old well house, the dungeon, and the tunnel which connected the two.

Yes...dungeon. Edith's family was your run-of-the-mill Lord Voldemort-type witches. You know, pure blood, dynasty, need a place to torture the muggles. OK...maybe not so outlandish, but the family made much use of that dungeon before the Witch Council and Order of Origin came to be, and humans were considered expendable—not to mention targets.

"He texted he had the map safe, and Adriana was nowhere in sight. So maybe she hasn't figured out our plans," I replied.

"We can hope," mumbled Edith.

Pulling into my driveway, I spied a familiar blue car next to Lorcan's truck but couldn't recall to whom it belonged.

I managed to take three steps in the direction of my back porch before two enormous shadows plowed into me, knocking me backward onto my butt.

"Max! Rex! Back off, you horrible brutes. I...no. Ack!"

Unless you've had the misfortune of having a facewash by hellhound saliva, you have no idea the horror I just experienced. Slimy sandpaper that smelled of death and peanut butter.

"Oh no! Who gave them peanut butter? Does no one understand how flatulent these beasts get on the stuff? They..."

BLAARP!

Too late. The green toxic fumes were all-encompassing, almost causing me to pass out cold.

"Whoa! What is that smell?" asked Andrea. She slammed the door of her Subaru and then paused to bury her face under the collar of her shirt.

Pointing to Max and Rex, I watched as understanding dawned. Andrea began rubbing her eyes and coughing.

"Ew! I can taste it. I'm eating dog fart!" Andrea cried. Running to the back door, she flapped her arms along the way in an ill-fated attempt to dissipate the funk.

Barreling into my home, we stumbled into the den to find Lorcan and Pandora entertaining a guest.

"Keisha! How are you? I thought I recognized your car."

"Lily. Hey, Andrea," she said.

Keisha had the impossible task of working as a nurse and companion for my Grandpa Antonio. Keeping an eye on his health and staying on top of his diet—and penchant for getting into trouble with his imaginary turf wars with several other centenarians running amok in our village, was almost a full-time job.

Antonio had a nasty habit of turning anyone who crossed him into farm animals.

"What brings you here? Is tonight your night off?" I asked.

"Adriana. Or rather, trying to stop her, anyway. I'm here to warn you Adriana intends to barge in on what I assume is a night of sleuthing," she informed us. "But I managed to beg off work tonight, claiming I had a massive migraine coming on which will prevent her from showing up here and tagging along with you."

"Keisha! You devil! I love it," cried Dorie.

I only felt mild pity for outsmarting Adriana. Despite her bravado, I knew she still had a long way to go before she would be back running at 100 percent and not feeling the effects of the attack. Thanks to Tiffany, Adriana took quite a hit of magic tainted with insanity. The clerics in charge of her recovery informed us there would be long-term effects, and she needed to slow down until the extent of the damage could be accessed. It had only been five months since the attack, and we were told it might take a year or more before she'd be her old self.

"While that's great news, now we are down one witch, and before you offer your services, Lor, you have that huge job tomorrow morning...early. Please don't ask me to not feel guilty if you stay out half the night helping us break into that compound."

"Like I won't worry half the night thinking about you breaking into that compound?" he replied with a smile. It made his laugh lines crinkle adorably, which often made me swoon.

"Look, Lily. You said yourself you needed four to do this tonight in case you had to call on elemental magic. North, south, east, and west...you won't be able to perform a spell without me."

"That's where you're wrong," cried Keisha, "Lily has a fourth witch."

"Who?" asked a puzzled Lorcan.

"Me!" Keisha swirled her hands in a "ta-da!" movement and her clothing transformed into what I could only describe as nighttime tribal wear.

"Keisha Holcomb! You look positively badass! Um...and I appreciate the offer, but you can do magic?" I stammered.

"So much so, you probably won't need this map!" said Lorcan, tucking it into a nearby kitchen drawer.

I knew Susanne's family had a low-level magical ability, Susanne being The Keeper of Tomes and all, but anything more substantial? Keisha is her niece...and Doc? I'd never seen the good vet do anything that smacked of magic.

"Girl. Don't let my nurse persona and staying off the witchy radar fool you. I'm lethal in the arcane arts."

"What's your specialty, Keisha? Are you a cleric? Potions and healing?" Andrea asked, assuming as we all did that her being a nurse must play into whatever talent was most prominent—despite the "lethal" comment.

"Conjuring," Keisha replied smugly.

"Conjuring?" I uttered, a bit confused as I couldn't fathom what creature or item Keisha could invoke.

Holding her hands out on either side of her statuesque frame, Keisha slowly began to chant, and within seconds, a four-pronged spear appeared in her left hand, and a ball of energy hovered over her right palm. She looked every bit like an African tribal goddess and rendered us speechless.

"Whoa. Wicked!" squeaked Andrea.

"You have no idea," chuckled Keisha with a wink.

CHAPTER 11

"*P*lease tell me your dad won't be upset with me for dragging you into my investigation?" I asked Keisha on our way to the Dietrich/Langsford estate.

"What he doesn't know won't kill him," Keisha responded with a tiny smirk. "Plus, if I informed him of my plans, I don't know how he would have handled it. I heard about your latest visit to his veterinary practice."

"Um...yeah...Wicked..."

"Yeah...heard it cost you," laughed Keisha. "Plus, you need me. My cousin, Rachelle, works as a maid for Wilhelmina. She promised to leave a key to the well house hidden outside for us."

That's right. In February, when we first attempted to gain entry to the estate, Susanne informed us that she had a niece employed there. A key would undoubtedly give us easy access, and perhaps our presence wouldn't trigger any alarms —magical or otherwise. Keisha thought of everything!

She was riding up front with me while Pandora and Andrea sat behind us, heads together, giggling. Edith said she'd meet us at her family's compound, which left the last and final member of this fellowship curled up beside me, snoozing away.

Wicked refused to be left behind, and I didn't try to lock her away to prevent her from following me. I mean, why bother? Somehow she managed to open doors and could even get into my Jeep at will. I wouldn't put it past her to drive it around town should she get the urge.

This time around, we chose our approach from the opposite end of the property, coming in from the side where it's wooded. We knew of a wonderfully concealed parking spot where we'd fought off a host of demons last time out, and I could only hope none would be waiting for us this go around.

After parking and locking my Jeep—not that it would do much good keeping anyone who wanted in from gaining entry—Jeep doors came off with a pin, after all—I pocketed my key. Motioning the others to follow me down a barely detectable path, we entered the woods.

We walked about one hundred yards or so and reached an eight-foot, black, chain-link fence that surrounded the wooded area of the estate.

"Are we going to climb it?" asked Andrea, glancing up.

"That's the only way we're getting in," I replied.

"Hang on a minute. I got this," stated Keisha.

Muttering under her breath and digging through the small pouch she wore strapped over one shoulder, Keisha came up with an item I wasn't expecting.

"Bolt cutters!" I exclaimed. "What kind of a Hermione Granger-type handbag is that?" I asked.

"Yeah. It is rather Wizarding World at that. I have an arsenal of tools at my disposal," said Keisha. "I conjured a few before we left your house. I need to be frugal with my magic expulsion, or I'll get too weak too quickly."

"Magic always comes with a price," intoned Dorie with a shrug.

Speaking of Dorie. Not one to be outdone with Keisha's display of magic and kickass ensemble, Pandora decided to conjure her own sleuthing outfit and now resembled a dominatrix ninja--all leather and mask. I'm not sure, but I think she might have a whip or flog of some sort tucked away until needed.

I could only hope and pray it didn't come down to her having to employ them. I couldn't imagine a scenario where she'd need them without blanching.

I had on the outfit my mother made for me, and it also felt a bit intimidating. With my hair up in a high ponytail, I resembled Lara Croft. But, with my dagger and various deadly magical darts tucked all over my person, I felt like her too.

Andrea was the only odd one, if you could call her that. She didn't look much like the three of us. Wearing jean shorts, a black tee, and sneakers, I wondered if she felt left out. Andrea rubbed bug repellant on her legs when we exited my Jeep and complained she'd probably get eaten alive by mosquitos, then glanced up to give us a wide smile. I assumed she felt like the odd duck in our group. That is until she pulled out her invisibility cloak and casually draped it over her shoulders.

Yes. Andrea has an invisibility cloak.

It makes her all kinds of cool in my book. Another badass witch.

I hadn't seen it since the first time I'd arrived in Sweet Briar, and something about it seemed different.

"It's more cape now...or throw," I stated, nodding to the item in question.

"I've woven it a bit bigger just for instances like this one. I figured, if all else fails, I can toss this over the four of us, and we'd be able to slip out of the compound undetected," Andrea beamed.

"What about if Wilhelmina or someone else casts a reveal spell? Won't they see through your magic?" asked Keisha.

"Nope," replied Andrea. "My magic is so potent even a revelation spell won't work!"

See? Badass.

Keisha's bolt cutter made quick work of the fence, and she opened a section just big enough for us to slip through. We didn't dare use magic this close to the house. The last thing we wanted was to trigger some kind of spell-detecting wards. We'd only use it from this point forward if absolutely necessary.

Keisha slipped through first, followed by Andrea and then Dorie, with me coming in the rear. Speaking of which...

"Dorie...did you forget underwear again?" I asked, exasperated yet grateful we were in the woods at least and not traipsing all over downtown in broad daylight. The men in town wouldn't be able to handle so much Dorie.

"Who wears underwear? I mean, really!" she drawled.

"Is that a tattoo?" I asked.

"What? Where? Oh...um..."

What's this? I've never once seen Pandora flummoxed, and here she was blushing over a wee little tattoo. It couldn't be that it was on one butt cheek...Dorie was no prude in hindsight.

Get it?

So, I wondered what had her so frazzled.

Peering at the spot and standing far closer than I would have preferred, all for curiosity's sake, I took a gander at the tattoo. I mean, I couldn't help it.

"Is that a werewolf? Since when do you have a thing for lycanthropes?" I asked.

"I do not have a thing for anything...or anyone. Mind your business."

Hmm...seems our crossroads demon doth protest too much. However, I didn't push it or call Dorie on her prickly retort. I needed her to focus on our task and not be a pouty brat. One with her nose constantly out of joint.

We stood at the edge of the woods and stared across the lawn at the mansion. Mansion was not the proper descriptor for such a hodgepodge of buildings. The main house could fit the bill, but it had so many attached outer facilities like the well house and what appeared to be an enormous garage, my mind went back to the tried and true "compound" I'd been using.

"What's that tower thingy in the distance? It's the only structure that appears to have a light on," I asked.

"Heh. That's Edith's old playhouse. I used to come here when I was younger before Dad had his fill of these folks," said Keisha morosely. "Those playdates were truly awful."

"I didn't know you and Edith were friends!"

"Friends? No. Forced playmates? Definitely. It was torture," said Keisha with a shudder.

"Edith hadn't used it in years, of course, but I heard rumors she allowed the neighborhood teens to hang out there smoking weed and getting up to no good," said Andrea. "Makes sense since she used them for nefarious reasons. So where is Edith anyway?"

Cautiously proceeding forward, we cut a path across the expansive lawn. Wicked kept pace and occasionally pounced on a cricket or grasshopper, her little butt wriggling right before she'd dive forward. I tossed an amused grin over my shoulder and noted Andrea's cloak was now flapped down around her shoulders, causing her to appear as if a disembodied head were floating along beside us.

"Get a load of that," snickered Dorie. "Andrea looks like the Headless Horseman."

"Wasn't he a body with a pumpkin for a head?" asked Keisha.

"No, he had a body with no head and rode a big, black horse. He carried a fiery pumpkin that he'd hurl at unsuspecting victims," explained Andrea.

"He still had a disembodied head," sniffed Dorie. "As much as I find this conversation fascinating, we need to lower our voices and find that key before we're discovered," she argued.

She was prickly indeed, considering she pointed out Andrea's floating head in the first place. I decided a long-overdue evening of drinks and girl talk needed to happen soon so I could suss the reason behind Pandora's cantankerous attitude. Meanwhile, I spied what appeared to be our key and addressed my group.

"It's right on the edge of that bench near the green door, and I'm certain everyone is fast asleep...I hear snoring. Don't you?"

Plodding along a few more paces, I noticed I'd gone ahead of the others without them following. I stopped to turn and see what was wrong.

"What?"

"Lily. How did you see the key from here?" asked Pandora.

"What do you mean how? It's right there on the...oh." Judging the distance from where we were standing, I realized there was no way I should have been able to see an object as tiny as a key, and in the dim lighting it should have been all but undetectable.

"I'm not sure. But I can see it plain as day," I mumbled. A lantern was on the corner of a potting shed beside the well house. It emanated just enough light to perhaps explain my ability to see the key. An elaborate greenhouse stuffed with all manner of plants, their heady scent reaching my nostrils, loomed beside it. My senses kept picking up something odd, and I went to mention it, but Pandora tapped me on the shoulder.

"And the snoring? My hearing is pretty stellar...but we're in the middle of an enormous lawn with the house quite a ways away. Even if we were right beneath a window, we'd still have a hard time hearing someone sleeping in an upstairs room," Dorie said, scrutinizing me like I'd morphed into a lab rat.

"Yowza! Look at Lily's eyes. They went black," whispered Andrea with a voice tinged with awe.

A weird sensation hit me at that moment, and my skin tingled, causing me to shiver.

"Lily...why are your teeth out?" asked Andrea, the strain evident in her voice.

"Teeth?"

"Fangs. Your fangs descended, woman!" Dorie rasped out.

A strange pulsing sound reached my ears, and I didn't reply, my attention hijacked by the sensation.

"Do you hear that? Forget the well house and dungeon. I don't sense any blood nor hear a heartbeat. Cornelius isn't there. What is that noise? Here...follow me."

I sprinted a few feet and turned to point out an odd tree that I suspected the vibration was emanating from. Imagine my surprise when I realized they were still a good thousand feet behind me, frozen in place. Trotting back to them, I asked what the holdup was, then observed their shocked expressions.

"Why didn't you follow me?" I asked.

"Follow you? Girl...we didn't even see you move. One second you were saying something about a noise, and the next, you were a blur of movement we couldn't track!" Keisha explained with a headshake.

"Lily Sweet! You've let your vampire out to play!" stated Dorie in admiration. "Look at you, all denizen of the night!"

I would have liked to respond that I'd not chosen to turn into a vamp nor realized the transformation had occurred. But just then, I launched into the air, flipped like a martial artist in one of those cheesy movies that I used to watch on Saturday mornings as a kid, and took down two guards who'd crept up behind my friends with guns drawn.

One good crack on their noggins was all it took, and the two toughs were knocked out cold, their guns dropped harmlessly by their sides.

"Toto? We aren't in Kansas anymore," whispered Andrea.

"That quote doesn't quite fit this situation, Drea," said Pandora. "It's more like 'something wicked this way comes.' And I don't mean the cat!"

It was a short-lived victory as a hoard of tiny imps flew out of the shed and began to attack us.

Keisha let loose her ball of light, which danced around the vicious buggers, taking a row of them out while she dodged and slashed an ancient-looking dagger around to defend her face.

Andrea ducked under the cloak and would toss an occasional slowing spell in their direction, which caused them to move in slow motion for a fraction of a second, just enough time for Pandora to zap them with her magic.

I used my dagger and took out a few, but they seemed to grow in numbers, and I didn't want to expend so much magic that those sleeping in the manor would awaken. So, we continued a relatively quiet battle, all things considered.

"They are trying to keep us from heading over to that tree," I breathed out, slapping down one imp who'd targeted my face.

"These pests are trying my patience," whispered Keisha, taking out another grouping who'd grabbed onto her braid, then began tugging them in all directions. Whatever that ball of energy she employed contained, it destroyed the imps but left her hair intact. A handy trick that!

Even Wicked was in on the action, pouncing and grabbing the minor demons and chewing them, then spitting out their tiny corpses. Her eyes were glowing in evil delight, and I'd never seen her so happy. A sleek black huntress taking down rampaging enemies with abandon.

It was the oddest battle ever. Tiny imps whose voices barely made a blip on the sound meter and the four of us with Wicked silently chopping and slicing our way through them.

Finally, their numbers dwindled, and the last group of demons came at us in one final surge, only to meet a magic sticky net that Andrea launched, ensnaring them in one fell swoop. Eradicating them was easy after that.

"That's it, ladies. They are all gone," I murmured, my fist in the air. "We make one heck of a team!"

"Yeah, and your eyes are still black as ink, and those fangs look lethal," giggled Dorie. "Lead on. Let's check out this tree of yours before the household wakes up!"

espite my little display of power and the fact I now resembled Mortimer more than I'd cared to, I managed to drag my companions over to the tree. After we bound and gagged the guards, we tossed them into the well house to ensure they were out of the way in case they awakened. I glanced at the key, which was indeed sitting on the corner of the bench, and we crossed the lawn, passing the greenhouse—me at a controlled pace this time—until we reached the foot of the gnarled old oak.

The vibration could now be felt and heard by all. Not to mention the strange smell I'd noticed earlier.

"And you sensed this from way over there?" asked Andrea. "That's fantastical!"

"It's not that far. You guys were focused on the shed...but the greenhouse and tree seemed to call at me. Now I'm a freak because of it."

I tried to retract my fangs several times, but they stubbornly remained extended. I think it had something to do with my inner alarm clanging loudly and my self-preservation refusing to allow me to proceed without a copious amount of caution.

"Do you not smell that?" I asked, sniffing every few seconds.

Dorie sniffed and shrugged. "Must be your shadowdancer coming out to play with your vamp, kiddo."

I wasn't sure about that, but I gazed at the tree and wondered if it was the source of the odor.

"Something evil is definitely in or around this tree. And I think it caused my vampirism to take over. I can't explain it. I certainly don't know how I'm doing any of this. But this tree is...it's...wrong."

Wicked strolled over to the tree's base and sniffed one of the large protruding roots. She puffed out her fur and growled but didn't seem afraid.

I think she still had one hapless imp in her mouth.

"What's wrong with the tree?" asked Keisha.

"I think it's alive. Or...duh, trees are alive, but not in the normal sense. What I mean is...this tree is aware. It's sentient. And I don't think it likes having us so near," I explained.

Keisha bravely walked up to the trunk and reached out her hand, placing it flat against the rough bark. "Holy moly! This tree is burning hot. There's no way any normal tree could be so heated unless it was burning."

Andrea and Pandora followed suit, touching the tree and finding it similarly heated.

"It's like touching what I'd imagine a charred hunk of firewood to feel like," said Andrea, pulling her hand away and checking it for burns.

There were none.

Needing to feel this phenomenon for myself, I walked up to the tree and ran my hand down the bark. No sooner than I did, a wailing alarm sounded from an unknown source, and a great rumbling shook the ground, almost knocking us off our feet. A few acorns dropped from the higher tree branches and pinged the greenhouse's roof.

"What the hell is that noise?" cried Dorie, no longer keeping her voice lowered.

"Oh, jeebers! Um, guys? We need to run...now!" I shouted, no longer worrying about waking up the household.

"What? Why? Oh!" Keisha turned to where I pointed and stumbled back a few steps.

Pandora and Andrea's eyes widened as four colossal Sentinels erupted from the ground and turned to face us.

"Well, crap," said Dorie. "One we could take. Maybe two. But four? I think I need to step in here because we will never make it back to your Jeep in time."

"So much for trying elemental magic. We won't last five seconds against those things," cried Keisha.

Before we could wonder what Pandora meant, she'd clasped hands with me and instructed the others to do the same. I called out to Wicked, who leaped upon my shoulders, and before you could say, "let's get the BLEEP out of here," Dorie transported us behind my Jeep, and we toppled over into a heap of tangled legs and arms.

"Hurry! No time for questions. Get it in the car and let's make tracks!" cried Pandora. I guess transporting us here wore her out.

No one argued. Within seconds, I'd reversed my vehicle and tore down the road back the way we'd come. It was only upon reaching the safety of town that we realized we were missing Wicked.

"Where is she?" I cried. "Didn't she get transported with the rest of us?"

I wrenched the shifter nob in reverse, preparing to head back to the Dietrich/Langsford estate, when my attention was distracted by the tiny figure of a woman dressed in a familiar scarf-laden outfit skulking around the corner of the gazebo in the center of the square.

Sitting on the street corner, staring directly at me, was none other than Wicked. How she managed to slip out of a moving Jeep in preparation to follow who could only be Adriana was beyond me. But that is precisely what she did. Turning on a dime with her tail held high, Wicked trotted after my great-grandmother into the darkness beyond the streetlamps that illuminated the gazebo.

What is that crazy old bat up to now? I thought to myself.

That's what I'm about to find out. Again, Wicked's internal voice came through loud and clear. And again, not one of my friends did anything to indicate they heard the furball...so I pointed out her retreating figure and that of Adriana's.

"Should we follow them?" asked Andrea.

"Ugh...no. I need food," cried Pandora.

"I think we should probably...hey! Is that Lorcan?" I cried, pointing to the sidewalk in the distance. It was dark on the opposite side of the square, with only a few lights illuminating certain spots on the walkway.

I would swear my fiancé shuffled across the corner near his shop to head off Adriana. Or was he meeting her?

"No. Let's see how that plays out. Wicked is on their trail."

With that, I put my vehicle in drive and continued down Main Street, then turned left on Wildflower Lane and home.

We let the hellhounds out to relieve themselves, drenching the yard as only massive hellhounds could, and I turned down the thermostat to make my house frigid. Giant canines, even of the demon variety, left behind quite a funk in the air and running the AC helped.

I stopped short when I saw what was left of my den.

"Wow," whispered Andrea in righteous awe of the devastation.

"They ate your sofa. And your armchair...and your other

armchair. You have no cushy seating left!" said Pandora needlessly, dropping to the floor in a heap.

"I'm going to kill them."

Keisha let loose a deep throaty laugh and patted me on the shoulder. "Ugh, I'm covered in imp goo and need a shower. What's our next move?"

"I need to find a way into that house to search for Judge Cornelius, and now I need to know what the deal is with that tree. But how to get past the Sentinels?" I asked. "And how come the Dietrich and Langsford clan have their own guardians? Why? What are they hiding?"

"Other than the judge? Who knows. But it makes you wonder," said Andrea.

Keisha was busy grabbing garbage bags and stuffing the copious amount of fluff into them, then moving on to the furniture pieces themselves. She then let two very guilty and subdued hellhounds back inside before they scratched my doors off.

"Into the sunroom with you both. Now!" I ordered.

Tails between their massive legs, Max and Rex slinked in that direction, pausing to sniff Dorie.

"I mean, I could use magic to try and repair these...or you can buy yourself some new furniture." Turning in my direction, Dorie managed to look mortified. "I will pay, of course."

"Will the magic in putting these back together be too much of a price?" I asked, resigned that I would likely be going furniture shopping with Lorcan the next day.

"Considering Max and Rex ate most of the fabric? I'd think so. I'd have to...um...extract it out of them magically, then clean the bits and pieces before stitching them together. Then I'd need to put it back the way it was."

"Save your magic and time," I sighed. "You're exhausted. I will head to Clayton in the morning."

"Fine by me," said Dorie, who quickly passed out on my

floor. Rex sniffed her face and managed to drool a puddle across it before I finally moved them into the sun porch.

I turned to survey my friends. "Ladies, thanks for the help tonight, even though we didn't get into the mansion. I'm not giving up, however."

Andrea began scratching her elbow, a sure sign she was worried. "They will know someone came on the property. The guards...and holy cow! We forgot them in the shed!"

"Nope. Pandora flicked an unbinding spell in their direction as we ran past," Keisha informed us. "They will wake up and mention four crazy women—well, three crazy women and one disembodied head. But they've never seen us before, so we can deny everything."

"Except we were accompanied by Wicked...we aren't going to fool anyone," I moaned.

"Let's not borrow trouble. We shall see what the morrow brings," said Andrea. "Too bad I forgot to hide all of us under my cloak!"

Pandora began snoring...loudly.

I had a feeling tomorrow would be one doozy of a day!

* * *

BEFORE TURNING in for the night, I text Lorcan to see if that was indeed him running after Adriana.

What's up?

I waited a few minutes, and then the telltale dots appeared, letting me know he was composing a reply.

Babysitting duty. Adriana suspected you were up to something and called me. I denied it, of course...

I waited for him to continue.

...somehow she convinced your cousin to stay with Antonio. Then she got into that death trap of a sedan and started driving all over town looking for you.

Great.

I texted a question to my honey and hoped he didn't have too much trouble with my formidable granny.

Did she give you much trouble? Are you home yet? Need me?

I rapid-fired one question after another at Lor, the guilt of causing him undue stress hiking my anxiety levels.

I always need you. Relax. Edith helped me cook up a plan and follow through with it.

That explained where my ghost buddy had been.

I may have hinted you were heading toward Nichols Pond, and she took the bait. You're in the clear, but she might show up at your place...

"And smack you around a little."

"Gah! What are you doing in my room? How did you get in here?" I cried, dropping my phone.

Adriana had been peering over my shoulder, spying on my texts.

She flicked her thumb at my bedroom window sitting open.

"I flew up on my broomstick."

"You did not."

"Did too."

"Did not because there is no such thing as a flying broomstick!"

Adriana's brown orbs lit with unholy mirth. "Care to make a bet?"

"I'm tired. I've had a long night. What do you want?"

"I want a great-granddaughter who appreciates me and doesn't sneak off on sleuthing missions without me for starters, leaving me to go on a wild goose chase with a spook."

Lovely. This would take some delicate backpedaling, or it would blow up to something more than it needed to be.

"I didn't leave you out of sleuthing..."

"Oh, so the three police cruisers called to the Dietrich estate just now had absolutely nothing to do with you then?" she asked.

"How could you know any police cruisers were out and about and heading to anyone's estate?" I asked, shocked that Adriana could know such a thing.

"Police scanner."

"What? How do you...where do you..."

"It's an App on my iPhone. Sheesh, Liliana. Get with the times!"

I was nonplussed. I also knew I was caught, and no amount of lying would do me any good. Even if I had the best intentions where Adriana's health was concerned, she would see through any lie, and the hurt would still be the result.

"I didn't want you to strain yourself. The clerics said you'd need more time to recover and..."

"Liliana. Do I look like someone who listens to clerics?"

I shook my head no.

"Do I look weak and frail about to keel over being so infirm?"

"No, but..."

"Did I not showcase my new summer sleuthing outfit, which can only mean I intended to do some summer sleuthing even though we are fast approaching autumn?" Adriana asked with one brow raised, arms crossed and fingers tapping on her elbows.

"You did..."

"I rest my case. You and your friends and that fiancé of yours purposely kept me away from the real action. And Lorcan is lucky I don't have the time to gather the ingredients needed to give him the world's worst case of jock itch."

Ack!

"Get some sleep. Tomorrow we are continuing this investigation. And I am leading the charge."

"Yes, ma'am. Um...why are you here? Was it just to rip me a new one?" I asked.

"I had to return your cat." Adriana pointed at my feet, and I jumped back when I realized Wicked was sitting there staring up at me. When did she show up? "She was trying to break into A Tale of Two Witches. We'll start there in the morning. Ciao!"

With that proclamation, Adriana sashayed out of my room and clomped down the stairs...I waited through the brief silence until I heard her slam my back door and the muffled woofs of greeting from my hellhounds before I let out the breath I'd been holding.

Adriana was pissed. She probably had a heap of hurt feelings, and I felt guilty, but I still knew I was not wrong in wanting to follow the clerics orders to a T. It could have been worse, and I guess starting at Hermione and Hortense Winters tea shop wouldn't be such a bad idea. At least I could start my morning off with a cup of some kind of magic elixir and a scone or two.

I picked up my phone, gave Lorcan an update, and wished him goodnight.

He texted back a kiss emoji.

"You could have given me a warning, you know," I grumped at Wicked, who'd jumped on my bed and began a full body wash.

I tried, but you didn't hear me. You need to speak with Hermione next.

"How are you doing that? Speaking in my head? Is it like what is happening to the others? Can you hear what they hear?"

I felt like a madwoman speaking to a cat who had both back feet in the air, proceeding to wash her tail, ignoring me.

"Fine! We'll go see Hermione."

Wicked sneezed.

Sighing, I made to crawl in bed with her, but then I remembered the open window. Yeah, right, Adriana flew up to my roof and climbed inside from there. Scampering back out of bed, I crossed the room and leaned forward to grab the nob to close my casement window and crank it shut. My eyes landed on a full-sized wood and straw broom lying innocuously on the shingles beneath the window.

"You've got to be kidding me!"

My text message alert sounded once more. Thinking it was Lorcan, I hurriedly glanced at the screen.

Adriana. She'd texted an emoji of a witch flying on a broom.

CHAPTER 13

"*E*arl Grey or Lapsang Souchong?" asked Hermione looking bedraggled and undeniably sleep-deprived as she held two different china teapots in either hand, blinking slowly like an owl.

"Earl Grey, please," I replied. "Hermione...is everything OK?"

Bottom lip trembling, Hermione glanced around, then set both pots on our table and shook her head slightly.

"No."

Hermione was subdued. Nothing like her usual bubbly self.

"I'm exhausted, Lily. I can't sleep most nights. The voices in my head...they never cease to stop calling me."

"That's just awful. Hey, can I have more tea? And I'd like another three scones and a crepe. I want the Crepe Suzette this time. Oh! You have banana nut bread. Bring it here. No...not a slice, the entire loaf," said Pandora between mouthfuls.

She'd arrived before us and began refueling her spent energy. Pandora did this with food. Lots and lots of food.

Hortense flew by and nodded at Dorie, placing a hand on Hermione's arm to let her know she was on it. A grateful Hermione slumped down in a free seat.

"Can you tell what they are saying?" Becky asked. Jake's girlfriend and the book shop owner had called bright and early and invited herself to breakfast when I explained where I was heading. Our party included me, Becky, Adriana, Pandora, and Andrea. None of us, except for Becky, seemed particularly awake, although, with every bite, Pandora seemed to perk up.

For once, Wicked remained content at home, sleeping in the early morning sunlight.

I think she'd had her fill of imp and needed to sleep off the caloric intake. Of course, it didn't help she'd hacked up a hairball at some time the previous night that looked suspiciously demonic.

"Not a thing. I just felt the urge to wander outside and found myself in the town square before I knew what was happening. I met Dennis and your father, Lily. They were ambling along, and we all stopped once we reached the fairgrounds."

"My dad?" Alarmed at the news, I tracked my eyes to Adriana to gauge her reaction.

"Where do you think I was heading when you drove past, Missy? And you better believe I noticed you." This she advanced to Pandora and Andrea as well. Andrea squirmed. Pandora just smirked, then continued shoving food in her face at rapid speed.

Just then, Shirley Jones walked into the tearoom looking like something that the proverbial cat dragged in.

"Shirley! How are you?" I asked.

Shirley was dressed in her EMT garb sporting her retro 70's beehive hairdo, and I was glad to see she at least tried to dab some makeup on. But it was restrained compared to how she usually appeared.

"Hiya, ladies. I could be better. I guess by now you've heard I'm among the afflicted."

Taking the seat at the table across from ours, Shirley placed an order for vanilla scones, a cheese Danish, and Irish Breakfast tea. "I was just outside speaking with poor old Chester Soule," she said.

Hermione sniffed at this pronouncement. The ongoing feud between sisters Hermione and Hortense, and siblings Chester and Hester Soule had become legendary in these parts, although no one knew the issue between them. She rose to place the order with Hortense, then wearily returned to her seat.

"I heard Chester hears the voices as well. Did he head out with the rest of you last night?" asked Andrea with a sympathetic tone to her voice.

"No. Hester chains him to his bed so he can't run off in the middle of the night and gives him a sleeping draught that seems to allow him some respite. He says he can still hear a faint trace of the voice, but the potion allows him to remain asleep. I think we all need some of what Hester has concocted," said Shirley woefully.

"Not unless you want to go insane or grow warts on your ears, you don't," sniffed Hortense, who'd just rejoined our group, having finished refilling teacups and bringing patrons their vittles. She plunked Shirley's order down in front of her and placed her hand on her hips.

"Those Soules are pills," she harrumphed.

That's right. The Winters sisters were adroit master potion makers. So why had no one thought to ask them to brew a concoction to aid the people suffering from this phenomenon?

"Hortense, can't you brew up a potion to aid everyone dealing with this problem?" I asked.

"Tsk, Lily. How can you ask such a thing? Do you know nothing of dark magic? And you are supposedly the greatest dark witch to come along in centuries!"

What did I say?

Pandora took pity on me and explained. "Without knowing what form of evil magic affects those hearing the voices, a potion could bring side effects...or worse, maybe permanent damage."

"Like...brain damage?" I asked breathlessly.

"Exactly," Dorie nodded, then peered out the window toward the funeral parlor. "Someone must stop Hester and her draught before Chester goes wonky."

"Like Liliana's base magic," snickered Adriana.

Hortense patted my head and placed my pumpkin scone in front of me. "Eat up, and don't let Adriana tease you. You've come a long way, and I'm sure you've improved by leaps and bounds."

"And burned Jeep seat cushions," added Adriana with an evil grin.

"Chester has been acting strangely. Joe at the diner called me at 5:00 a.m. knowing I'd be up early waiting on a special delivery at my shop," said Becky, "and he said he found Chester outside the diner speaking to the air. Like having a full-on conversation with nothing."

"Big deal. Chester probably was chatting with a ghost or two," said Adriana. "Nothing new there."

"No. Joe asked him what the matter was, and Chester jumped a mile into the air and then screamed at Joe to mind his business. Joe tried to calm him down, but Chester said the voices needed him to fetch the boys and bring them home!" stated Becky breathlessly. "Then Chester ran off to the funeral home and went inside, leaving Joe to scratch his head. What do you think he meant by that? Fetch the boys?"

"Look! There's Chester now," cried Dorie. "I'm going to head outside and speak with him. We can't have him going insane...er...more insane now, right? I'll try to get some answers."

Pandora stood and rushed out of the tea shop with all eyes tracking her progress. She ran across the street and nearly caused three separate car accidents. Not because she'd jaywalked—which she did, mind you. Today, Dorie chose to wear white short shorts that would make Daisy Duke blush. Her top was a matching too-tight white shirt whose buttons strained to the point of flying off and taking out the nearest passerby with deadly precision.

It didn't help that she'd worn a bright red bra and panties that could be seen through the top and bottom fabric. Hey...at least today she'd remembered undergarments!

"That demon is a menace!" mumbled Hortense.

"You're just jealous because every man in a hundred-mile radius is smitten with her and not you," laughed Hermione before the grin faded from her careworn face. The woman needed some solid sleep, and soon!

"If you weren't so ill, I'd tell you to bite my sweet little behind, Sissy. You've been a real pain in the butt since this started," cried Hortense, who flounced into the kitchen to continue food preparations.

"Little. Her butt hasn't been little since it was in diapers," joked Hermione half-heartedly.

Trying to gain some control of the conversation, I chose to ask Hermione and Shirley more questions, not that I thought they had anything new to impart.

"I hope Chester isn't losing it. The poor guy is weird enough without going insane over this plaguing nuisance. "This voice, or voices...is there nothing you can make out?

Anything that would indicate whether it was male or female...or if it seems familiar?"

Adriana looked at me in approval.

"That's a good question, Squirt. Does anything about it seem recognizable, ladies?"

Hermione shook her head no, but Shirley hesitated and bit her lip before dropping her head.

"What is it, Shirley? What's wrong?" I asked.

"Lily, remember a few months back when you confronted me and asked what was bothering me because I looked like a frazzled chicken running amok?"

I smiled and nodded yes, indicating she should go on. "You told us you were guilty about speaking to Alan and giving out information he might have used..."

"No! Not that. Yes, I was upset about that faux pas. But...I held back even more info, ladies. You see...I've heard the voices since back then."

"What?" cried Andrea and Hermione at the same time.

"And you didn't tell anyone?" barked Adriana unkindly.

"I was so afraid I'd lose my job! I need this job, Adriana. Not everyone has a family trust they can rely on, you know!" Shirley made to stand and leave, but we settled her back down, and I tossed Adriana a warning glare not to rattle the poor woman any further.

"No one could blame you, Shirley. I can't imagine what you've been going through. It must be frightening not understanding where these voices are coming from or what it all means."

"I'll tell you what it means."

We collectively turned to the new voice who'd uttered that statement to find the daunting figure of Wilhelmina Dietrich standing at the entrance to the tea shop. She looked ready to spit nails and take no prisoners.

Pointing a gnarled finger in my direction, Wilhelmina raised her voice in accusation.

"You need to be arrested, Lily Sweet. Don't even deny that you and your ragtag group of demented friends trespassed on my property last night. One of my guards identified you from a photograph, and I've called for your arrest! This dark witch must be behind the voices...only she can create a spell so vile."

"Oh, stuff it, Willie. Lily was with me last night. She had to help me pry my broom loose from her roof...I got it stuck up there on a routine flyby," Adriana shot back.

Wilhelmina paid her no mind and crossed the room to lean her massive bulk over me while I forced myself to not cower in her presence.

"Not only am I calling for your arrest, I've already petitioned the Council to strip you of your Elder status and bring you to trial for treason!"

Well, that's a bit harsh.

CHAPTER 14

*J*ake met us by the elevator. He was standing with his hands behind his back, wearing a gorgeous Armani suit and designer glasses that gave him a sultry appearance. Jake always seemed more like a model and less like an attorney. His nose wrinkled when he saw us, then he extended a hand and indicated we should follow him down a nearby hallway. The scowl on his face was pronounced.

"Nice to see you looking so well, Adriana," he addressed my great-grandmother thusly. Then Jake quickly greeted everyone before turning to me.

"Lily."

OK. Me, he wasn't so thrilled to see.

Accompanying me were Adriana, Lorcan, Andrea, and Uncle Owen. The latter looked resigned but calm. I wanted to question everyone, but when I tried to speak, Jake signaled for me to remain quiet.

Fine. Be that way.

We followed Jake from the elevator down an airy hallway to an expansive conference room, a partitioned-off office with a large desk in the corner. "This is my office here at the Witch Council," he said as he led us to it and offered us seats in front of his desk. It definitely wasn't an office, at least not in my book. A proper office needed its own walls, a door, and, more importantly, privacy. Instead, this was an over-sized impartial mega-cubicle. As we walked through, we passed two severe ladies huddled together around a computer, who gave us curious, if not downright hostile glances.

"Morning," I murmured.

Unfriendly nods in reply. The grand inquisitors, I presume.

The Sweet Briar police were not even called to arrest me. Instead, a minion from the Witch Council arrived on the heels of Wilhelmina and placed magical cuffs around my hands to nullify my magic and lead me away like a common criminal.

OK. I trespassed on private land I accosted two guards and slew a hoard of demons. But I'm not a criminal! I'm innocent! Except I really did do those things. Ugh. I didn't want to sound like every loser that ever got arrested claiming innocence.

"I didn't do anything wrong! I'm innocent. Jake, you have to help me here!"

OK, fine. I'm a loser.

Again, Jake raised his hand to silence me, and I gritted my teeth in frustration. Finally, Lorcan placed a hand on my shoulder and squeezed, offering comfort. "Hang on, Lily. Jake gave me a slight nod and barely a wink. I'm not sure what's going on but listen to him, OK?" he whispered, then kissed my temple.

Grr. I wanted to lash out at everyone present but swallowed my pride and remained quiet.

A commotion back at the elevators heralded the arrival of

Wilhelmina and her band of merry executioners. This was going to suck chunks.

"There she is! Trying to hide behind an attorney. Well, it won't work this time!" cried Wilhelmina, waving her chubby index finger at me.

"Woman! Stop your blathering and go sit down!" snapped Adriana. "Before I turn you into a worm for annoying my eardrums."

"Threaten me, Adriana, and you might be next. Your dynasty is coming to an end on this day, and there is nothing you can do to stop it," crowed Wilhelmina with a gigantic grin that caused her to resemble a giant toad that just swallowed a juicy fly.

"Really? I could say the same to you, Willie. And would you care to explain why you have four Sentinels roaming your grounds?" barked Adriana.

"If your Antonio could conjure a set of his own, there was no reason why Boris and I couldn't do the same. You don't get to make your own guardians, and the rest of the witch folk are banned," sniffed Wilhelmina.

"Ah! Tammy and Estelle! So nice to see you ladies. Here is the criminal. Take her away!" Wilhelmina turned to smile at her posse, which consisted of her husband, Boris, a woman I recognized as Julia Crawley, and a few of her busybody cronies who were all members of the families currently plotting against mine. In other words, the usual bunch of nasty loons.

Wilhelmina clasped her hands, rubbing them together like someone dropped a tasty treat in front of her and addressed everyone present. "Let's get this over with so I can celebrate with my family," she commanded.

The two women who'd ogled me when I'd first arrived seemed more perturbed by Willie than they had been antagonistic when I greeted them. I stood and faced them, my hands still trapped by the cuffs, and I wanted to plead my case...however, I knew enough to keep my trap shut and allow Jake to do his thing.

Here goes nothing.

"For heaven's sake. Why is Lily in cuffs? Is this some kind of joke?" In walked Tanaquil Alessi, my mentor and friend, followed by Gloria Stillwell and Olivia Ogden-Meyers. All Elders...and none pleased to find me compromised by shackles.

"Joke? She's a criminal. I filed a complaint with the Council and have papers drawn to have her incarcerated, stripped of magic, and locked away for trespass and assault," cried Wilhelmina.

"What are you talking about, Willie? Lily is no criminal." Olivia waved her hands, and I felt the cuffs loosen and then drop to the floor at my feet. "Jake, dear, be a good boy and pick those up and give them to Johnathan."

A young man I'd not noticed stepped forward to take the cuffs from Jake, and I recognized him as the one who'd shackled me in the first place. He wouldn't meet my stare and was a furious shade of red. The poor man looked like he wanted a hole to open in the floor to swallow him up. There sure was a lot of that going around here lately.

"What is this treachery? Stop it. This woman is a thief! A scoundrel!"

Hey. I didn't steal anything. And a scoundrel? Not to be sexist, but can women even be scoundrels? I thought that descriptor was left to the males. But what did I know?

"Nonsense. Lily is none of these things. Now...I'm glad you are here, Wilhelmina and Julia. You can sign the papers and be on your way. You obviously missed the call to convene yesterday afternoon, and yours are the only two signatures I have left to add to the official decree," stated Tanaquil delicately.

"Decree? What decree? I was busy in Atlanta yesterday and couldn't make the meeting," Willie looked apoplectic, and the vein on her forehead throbbed viciously. Someone needed to grab her a chair before she keeled over. Heck, I could use one too, because I was dizzy with worry and fearful this would descend into battle should my friends try to free me in some underhanded way. "Lily is under arrest!" this came out weakly as uncertainty filtered into Wilhelmina's bearing.

I don't know what my friends were attempting, but let's face it. The guards identified me. I'm toast.

"Don't be silly, woman. What could Lily possibly have done to you to wrongly accuse her of such nonsense?" asked Gloria. The steel in her voice contrasted sharply with a now sputtering Wilhelmina.

I noticed Julia take a surreptitious step away from the woman. Boris just sighed and looked at his feet.

"I don't understand. Lily was identified as being on my property last night. She accosted my guards and set the Sentinels off, causing utter chaos. She needs to be incarcerated."

"Lily wasn't trespassing! How bizarre you should say this," smiled Olivia with subtle malice.

"But..."

"How can the Head Investigator be trespassing when she was doing what she is appointed to do? Investigate!" asked Tanaquil to no one in particular.

I watched as the two women, Tammy and Estelle, opened the folders they'd been carrying and set paperwork down on the table. Then, taking out a pen, one of them placed it near the paperwork and motioned for Wilhelmina and Julia to come forward to sign.

"I don't understand," Willie repeated. I began to feel sorry for the woman because even addled with worry, I understood the sneaky and underhanded bit of trickery my friends procured, and boy, was I grateful.

It seems somehow, and without my knowledge, a meeting was called yesterday to rush the vote among Elders to make me Head of Investigations and to ensure the petition to make me Head of Oddities was locked away with Jerry all day.

Spinning to face Adriana, Willie screeched, "You did this!"

"Well, now, I'm not sure why all the fuss. You were the one who wanted to rush the vote and make Liliana Head of Oddities. I complied with your hurried timeline and asked for the vote and tally to happen yesterday evening. Everyone voted. Unfortunately, no one chose Oddities except for Stella."

Her daughter and Edith's mother.

"Wait. The others, my friends...Boris!" Turning to confront her spouse, Wilhelmina found the mild-mannered man in question shrugging and unapologetic.

"It made more sense for the girl to be Head of Investigations. She always snoops around town and has a knack for discovering answers," he stated.

"But...but...she was on our property!" Wilhelmina was incensed and outraged at this turn of events and by the betrayal of her own spouse. I didn't envy Boris.

"And if you have nothing to hide, you won't be in trouble if she is...right, dear?" asked Olivia. "Lily has reason to be on your property. I have been trying to reach Judge Dietrich to no avail. She was only doing a well-person check.

"He's fine. Wilhelmina told us she sent him to our hunting lodge to see if the voices wouldn't bother him up there...the coverage is iffy. I can drive up and get him if you'd like, Olivia," offered Boris.

"That would be lovely. Do you have something to add, Wilhelmina?" Olivia addressed the woman who had just developed a facial tic.

Clamping her mouth shut and turning on her heel, Wilhelmina Dietrich stormed from the room, the rush of air knocking the papers off the table and scattering them this way and that.

"Signatures! We need them!" Tanaquil shouted at her retreating back. "Well...no matter. Boris was enough to lock Lily in as Head of Investigations. Congratulations, Lily!" she said with a smile.

"When did you manage to get this done? I thought..."

Pausing, I waited for Boris and those following Wilhelmina to clear the room, but I noticed Julia Crawley had remained behind.

Stepping forward tentatively, she reached her hand out to me and in fumbled speech, pleaded that I look into her troubles. "The voices, Lily. They are driving me insane. Can you please investigate and find out who or what is behind it?"

How do you like this turn of events?

* * *

"GRAND INVESTIGATOR! You're a rock star, Lily," said Andrea.

"Head Investigator. There's nothing grand about it," I laughed, thrilled to have a team of people around me who not only looked out for me but cared enough to do so.

"Willie's blood pressure must be at the boiling point," cackled Adriana wickedly. "Did you see her flapping those gums? She looked like a fish stuck out of the water!"

Knowing full well Adriana was behind the vote being cast quickly and before she became aware I'd planned on going to the Dietrich/Langsford estate, I knew I owed her a big one.

We were gathered outside the Witch Council near a fountain whose waters bubbled and danced, the noise drowning out any nearby conversations. Before changing my mind, I walked up to my great-grandmother and hugged her tight.

"Thank you."

"What's this?" she asked with a wry grin.

"Gratitude. Thank you for looking out for me," I said, tearing up.

"Not bad for an invalid too old and feeble to get on any longer."

"You know I didn't mean to leave you out. I'm only worried about your health. Seeing you lying there helpless when you were attacked...I just..."

"It's OK, Cara. I understand. It doesn't mean I have no intention of sleuthing along with you now that you are official and all," Adriana said with delight.

"Just think! You can really and truly investigate if you should discover another dead body or trip over one anyway," cried Andrea.

I shuddered and gave my cousin an incredulous look.

"Andrea! Bite your tongue. The last thing I'd ever want is to find another dead body. Or skeleton. Or anything undead...and that includes ghosts!"

We moved toward the parking lot, but I reached out and grabbed Adriana's arm.

"Isn't that Lowell Hickinbottom? Do you know him? He works at the fairgrounds."

"Yes, that is him. Why?" replied Adriana.

"According to Pandora, he's also suffering from hearing voices."

I rushed over to where the man was walking and addressed him. "Lowell? Hey...hi. Um, do you have a minute?"

Eyes wide and bloodshot as all get-out, Lowell Hickinbottom looked like he hadn't slept in decades. A shell of a man who once appeared a thin but healthy groundskeeper. Forget the cryptwalker business for a minute; the man already looked like a corpse. Walking dead perfectly described Lowell.

"Can I help you, Miss Lily?" he asked gravelly.

Miss Lily. Oh, I liked him already. No one ever addressed me as such.

"Are you OK?"

"Heh. OK? Not really. Haunted? Do you know what it's like to hear voices telling you to dig up the entire cemetery and prop the bodies outside their graves? I'm about to go mad trying to ignore them."

"What? You can hear the voices clearly?" cried Adriana. We only know of one other person who can tell what they're saying—allegedly—and that's Judge Dietrich. Do you mean to tell me you can as well?"

"Well, yeah," replied Lowell, seemingly confused. "And sometimes it's just *voice*. One."

"My good man! Did you not think to tell someone about this?" This was from my Uncle Owen, who seemed to want to throttle poor Lowell and was doing everything in his power not to.

"I'm sorry. I can't even think straight. I assumed everyone else could hear what it said. I was just heading inside to tell Olivia Ogden-Meyers I can't perform my duties any longer and need to go see one of the cleric shrinks."

"You need to head to the hospital, Lowell...and allow the clerics to try some potions that might ease the voices from taunting you," said Adriana gently. "Or you can come to my home, and I can see what I can cook up in my cauldron and then you can stay for lunch. My family is gathering there now, and we can talk further. We need to know what the voice...or voices are telling you."

"If you think that's a good idea, I'm for it, ma'am. But I think I'd much rather go to the hospital. Or...no. No! NO! I need to leave. Now!"

Turning the way he had come, Lowell ran off at a sprint, holding his head and moaning before anyone could react.

"Wait! Lowell...get back here!" exclaimed Adriana. It was all for naught—who knew cryptwallkers could cover such a distance in so short a time?

A resounding clang shattered the relative peace, and Edith popped an inch from my nose.

"Yikes! Woman! What is wrong with you?" I'd asked her to give me a warning before showing up and scaring the bejesus out of me, but now I'm thinking the loud bangs or ringing had to be worse.

"Lily! Come quick. Hurry! Your mom is frantic. Charlie has gone missing and so has Dennis. June is crying and moaning something awful."

"What? Where is she...Adelaide? And June?" Adriana motioned for Lorcan to get his truck.

Jake ran up to us, waving his phone. "My mom is hysterical. Dad's gone missing. Someone reported he was walking down Main Street heading to his shop when a dark sedan pulled up, grabbed him, and drove off."

A dark sedan? Who could pull a grown man off the street like that?

What on earth was going on around here?

CHAPTER 15

Screeching to a halt outside June's Emporium, we found Pandora and my mom comforting June with...Nora? My obstinate cousin was the last person I expected to see with my mother, let alone Pandora.

June seemed to be stumbling over her words while giving information to Sheriff Glen Buford. I'd not see the officer in a few weeks, and he'd lost quite a lot of weight. Assisting the sheriff was the newest deputy to replace a long list of bad ones in recent months. This one, a man, looked less hostile than the previous three, if that were possible.

I didn't have a good track record when it came to the deputies in this town.

"Lily! Oh, thank goodness you're here. Something horrible has happened," cried Adelaide.

"Mom, what's wrong? I heard Dad is missing and Dennis was abducted?" I asked, hopping out of my Jeep with Andrea right behind me. Adriana arrived with Lorcan, and we pestered the sheriff to discover what had happened.

June ran over and threw her arms around me, which set my old reaction of awkwardly stiffening up to return. All I could do was pat her back, feeling inadequate and inept. I've done better since living among family and friends who could express their emotions and be demonstrative after an entire early life of never daring to hug my Aunt Jessica who wasn't the touchy-feely type.

"Charlie left this morning saying he needed to meet up with Dennis, who'd called leaving a message. I just played it for Glen, and it's disturbing. Dennis sounds deranged...mumbling about meeting the boys. Now he's disappeared, and someone drove off with Dennis seemingly a hostage!"

I noticed Maureen inching her way in our direction and became annoyed. I didn't need the girl to pester us now...nor listen in and get fodder for the gossip mill.

However, I didn't have time to say anything because Adelaide continued with her story.

"By the time I arrived, June was frantically running up and down the street calling out to anyone for help."

"They took him! They took my Dennis. Jake! Jake...they took your father!" June noticed Jake's arrival and rushed over to throw herself in his arms, dragging me along with her. I was starting to feel like a tug toy in a dogfight.

"OK, everyone. Settle down. I need more information if I'm going to be able to investigate this," shouted Sheriff Glen in an attempt to gain control over the situation.

"What's going on in this town anyway? This is your fault, Glen, for hiring a string of inept deputies. Now we have a reputation for being soft...or corrupt," argued Adriana.

And control went out the window.

"Now, Adriana, you can't..."

"Yes, I can!"

"Dennis! My Dennis!" wailed June.

"I was at the café and saw a speeding car almost run Dennis over. I came running to offer my help when I saw he'd been taken," Nora offered.

"You're just trying to brown nose yourself back into the family." Pandora taunted my cousin, rolling her eyes at the audacity. I wanted to tell Dorie to cut it out and give Nora the benefit of the doubt, but she flicked Nora on the ear and then stomped over to June for a hug, pulling her off me.

"I thought you went after Chester Soule?" I whispered.

"I did, but he took one look at me and ran off screaming about getting the lads and climbing the tower. The man has gone nuts. Well, er...nuttier," Pandora whispered back. "And you won't believe this. But Adelaide said a witness saw Lowell Hickinbottom tearing down the street chasing after the sedan!"

"Who's the witness?" I asked.

Pandora just shrugged.

"We need a search party!" sobbed June.

"We need the police! We need..."

"Mom! Settle. The police are here. Everyone needs to calm down!" Jake declared, awkwardly patting his mom while running one hand through his hair. Calm, Jake?

I could see he was frantic with worry, and his mom's anxiety wasn't helping at all. Becky came running across the square to throw herself at him in a grand display of support, which seemed to settle Jake's nerves ever so slightly.

Lorcan glanced at me and shrugged, then began placing his hands on the most excitable in the group, whispering words of comfort. Instantly, the noise level lowered as his empath magic coursed through those gathered.

Edith followed along behind him, pausing to address me.

"I'm sorry I didn't show up at my family estate. Lorcan..."

"Explained everything to me. Thanks for helping with Adriana, Edith," I responded. Edith smiled, then floated near my mom, who could see and hear her. They bent their heads together and began commiserating with one another.

While this was going on, Maureen managed to catch my eye and motioned me over.

Now what? I thought irritably.

"Um...hey."

Really? I have a family emergency, and this idiot hits me with a bland greeting.

"Maureen, I don't have time for..."

"I saw what happened. And I think I know who took Dennis. Look...I filmed it on my phone and..."

"And you didn't tell anyone? What's wrong with you?" I yelled.

"Lily. Quiet down. If you'd just listen to me, I'm trying to tell you something."

In a bold move for someone I considered a marginal enemy, Maureen reached out and grabbed my top pulling me close. "Quiet. Just look and you will see why I didn't say anything yet."

Speechless but nonetheless curious, especially in light of Maureen's bold actions, I peered at the screen on her phone...and all the color drained from my face.

I watched as a large, charcoal grey Lincoln came flying down Main Street toward the Emporium with Dennis ahead of it, jogging down the sidewalk. You could see the car getting closer and veering to the curb. A man got out of the car's passenger side, then ran up to Dennis, and seemed to forcibly walk him over to the passenger back seat. The driver was indistinguishable at first. I could just make out a third person sitting behind the driver, who remained concealed by the glare from the windows. However, two things caused me to realize something horrible was going down.

One...the vehicle belonged to my great-grandparents; it was Antonio's old Lincoln. And two...the man who kidnapped Dennis was none other than my dad, Charlie Sweet.

This was not good.

"I'm sorry. I didn't want to upset your mom after everything she'd been through, and June is beyond consolable. I didn't know what to do! I figured you'd be here...I mean, you always turn up to investigate these things. I just didn't know what to do! I tried calling you, but it kept going to voice mail," Maureen sniveled, and I instantly felt remorse. The girl was trying to help, and I let my prejudice get in the way. She couldn't know I'd had to turn off my phone while embroiled in Council business.

"No. I'm sorry. Thank you for thinking to keep this from the police...for now, anyway," I began, but Maureen cut me off again.

"Wait. There's more, Lily. I know who the driver is."

Whoa. I did not see that coming.

"Tell me, Maureen. Please," I implored.

She finagled some more with her phone, the apparent witness to the incident.

Ten seconds after the car sped off down the road, the figure of Lowell Hickinbottom could be seen giving chase.

"The driver was Chester Soule...and Hester was in the back seat," cried Maureen, "And what's more...they have Wicked!"

* * *

I WAS MOMENTARILY STRUCK speechless by this announcement and remained blinking like a fool for thirty seconds before I exploded. This instantly quieted the entirety of the citizens in my group. Those who'd come outside homes and businesses to gawk and listen murmured amongst themselves.

When I'd informed everyone of what Maureen told me, the ensuing hoopla took hours to settle, and an all-out search began in earnest. Volunteers popped up out of the woodwork and offered their services. Brian got the paranormal sector of the state police involved and amateur to professional, we searched day and night for any sign of that car and our friends and family to no avail.

They seemed to have disappeared into thin air.

I was only mildly alarmed at Wicked having been taken along with the runaways—I didn't know how else to think of them at this point—since, even in their trauma-plagued misery, I couldn't imagine a reason they'd hurt her. I had hoped she'd reach out to me telepathically like she'd been doing in recent weeks...but nothing.

Now you go silent, cat?

Everyone in town assumed the police and even my family would quickly get to the bottom of this disturbance and the disappearance of our loved ones. But as the weeks went by, faith dwindled along with any hope of discovering where they'd gone. Or what had caused them to run.

"We should have canceled the Fall Fun Festival," grumbled Adriana. She and my mom seemed to be suffering greatly— and who could blame them? We'd just gotten my dad back after decades of drama, and now he's gone again. And this time of his own volition it seems!

"We have too many vendors who'd paid ahead. Our crisis shouldn't cause the loss of income for so many of our artisans and small business owners. If we had canceled," I explained while trying to untangle one of my windchimes that managed to become ensnared in the cool autumn breeze, "they would be hurting."

Adriana frowned but didn't argue with me further. I'd stayed glued to my great-grandmother, leaving much of the investigating to Dorie and my friends. She needed me, and I needed to be at the Fall Festival manning my booth. I didn't have a choice since I was one of the organizers of this year's event. Even Tanaquil and Gloria were here doing the same. It certainly put a damper on any kind of manhunt.

September spilled into October. My dad and the rest missing five weeks now with no news and no contact of any kind, left a pall over us all. Things sure looked bleak.

I worked my booth, and business was brisk. Unaware of our hardship, happy tourists came in droves to shop in the witchy village and partake of the festive offerings. Sweet Briar was making some serious bank.

"Cousin Fiona will be here tomorrow to take over the booth so I can continue my search," I informed Adriana lamely. It's not like weeks of doing just that amounted to much. I felt like a failure, even though I knew I was being ridiculous. I felt guilty about making a profit while we had missing loved ones. Despite my tireless searching and brainstorming, I couldn't help but blame myself and worried I might be the cause. I knew I was missing something, and I couldn't shake the nagging thought all this had something to do with me.

Pandora said I was projecting, whatever that meant.

"You're taking on the blame because you're used to every moment of evil and mayhem to strike this village be about you," she explained. "Understandable, because for a while, it was about you. That doesn't mean it's the same this time."

Tell that to my conscience!

Now, glancing around the heavily decorated fairgrounds, Halloween décor splashed on every window, front stoop, booth, banner, and even the surrounding trees, I silently lamented yet another October 31st without me enjoying it due to an unknown terror.

And boy, did I resent it.

To top it off, I was concerned Adriana had been pushing herself to the limit and beyond. Her face remained strained and pale, and she was a shell of her former self.

"I'm going to head home now. Antonio doesn't want me away too long. He's..."

Shaking her head and hunching over, my great-grandmother started to walk away from my booth. I stopped her with a hand on her arm as she passed.

"I've got this. I will not let my first official case as Head Investigator fail. Not when it's my dad and friends who are in trouble. I promise you."

Patting my hand and managing a wan smile, I watched as Adriana slowly walked out of the fairgrounds and over to her car, then drove off. A tiny, broken woman who'd aged these last few weeks. Worry would do that to you.

I became enraged and tossed the offending windchime aside, causing a tourist next to me to cry out in fear.

"I'm so sorry! I didn't see you there."

The woman harumphed and strode away quickly, occasionally peering over her shoulder to see if I'd give chase like the raging lunatic I must appear to be.

Sighing, I decided I'd had enough for the day and began counting receipts and shutting down the booth.

"Closing early?" Pandora, appearing at my side unexpectedly, cause me to jump. My heart racing, I sympathized with the woman I had just startled.

"Yes. I can't stay here a minute longer."

"I get it. Let's go for a ride. Get those detective juices flowing," suggested Dorie.

While I didn't want to ride around aimlessly, I knew I had to do something or I'd go mad.

"What do you have in mind?" I asked.

I usually tried to humor Pandora unless her ideas were beyond the pale...even for a demon. But it couldn't hurt to see what she had up her sleeve.

"Oh, nothing much. But I think it's time we tried something a bit different, even for us," replied Dorie cryptically, and she wouldn't explain further, no matter how much I pestered.

Fine. Be that way. I could wait and see.

Maybe.

Not.

CHAPTER 16

*A*fter commandeering my Jeep and allowing Dorie to drive around town, we turned down a picturesque street. She was singing off-key at the top of her lungs while blasting music so loudly I feared my speakers might blow. Finally, we pulled up to a tiny gingerbread cottage, all pink with white trim. It was adorable and not too far from my grandparent's neighborhood.

I didn't want to admit to her that singing along to my favorite tunes and wasting gas was just what I needed to bring me out of my funk. But now, sitting outside a strange house, I felt my anxiety growing once more.

"Where are we?" I asked. "Who lives here?"

"You'll see," trilled Dorie, hopping out of my vehicle and marching up the beautifully landscaped front walk.

Ringing the doorbell, we only had to wait seconds before it was thrown open, and a scowling Valerie Parks stood on the other side of the screen door from us.

"What do you two want? And please tell me your evil feline isn't with you. My chihuahua will piddle everywhere if he gets anxious."

Didn't all chihuahuas piddle at will whether or not they were upset? I thought it went hand in hand with the Breed. Like a requirement for being tiny and vicious, the excessive spreading of yellow stains everywhere was the norm.

"No. Um...she's away." I felt a sob lodge in my throat. For all her idiosyncrasies, I missed my girl something fierce.

"We came to hire you for a séance or something. I'm not sure what you'd call it," said Dorie. "A divination? Maybe. Anyway...we need you."

"No."

That came quick and belied an argument.

"What do you mean, 'no?' You do this for a living!" cried Dorie.

"I do this as a side gig. And I don't often perform for those in the Breed. I'm more sideshow and less psychoanalyst. If you need love advice, see a potions master for one of their concoctions."

Making to shut the door, Valerie was surprised when Pandora quickly opened the screen and stopped her from doing so with a well-placed foot on the threshold.

"Wait just a minute, vet lady. We need your brand of woo-woo, and I for one, won't take no for an answer."

Valerie smiled tightly but didn't budge. "Well, I hate to be a disappointment to you, but the answer is still no."

* * *

"You kidnapped her. Oh my gosh, Pandora! What is *wrong* with you?" I cried, peering at my rearview mirror as Dorie rode in the back with a bound and gagged Valerie Parks seething on the seat next to her.

I was driving the getaway car because, yes...who else would? And really, what choice did I have once Pandora used demon magic on the woman? In seconds, we had a prone if irate, victim and a crossroads demon hoisting said victim over her shoulder like she'd done this a million times.

And who knows? Knowing Dorie, maybe she had!

"I didn't know you were so strong. But despite that...this is wrong. We could have explained our situation to Valerie and our needs. You went and kidnapped her instead. What if the neighbors saw us?"

"Magic. OK...I might be stronger than your average female, but I used the teensiest bit of magic to bolster my strength." Pandora began bragging like she'd just bagged a stag or something. This was a side of the woman I'd hoped never to see again.

"But..."

"But nothing. We need this witch, and now we have her. Just drive to your place so we can move on to phase two."

Phase two? Somehow I assumed Dorie was making this up as we went along. Who knew she had a phase two? Please don't make there be a phase three...or four!

I reached home in record time and found Andrea and Keisha waiting for me. Finally! Some help to convince Pandora to turn herself in and beg Valerie not to press charges.

"Quick. Bring Valerie inside, Pandora and put her in Lily's office," instructed Keisha.

What?

Had everyone gone mad without me knowing?

"Keep the gag in her mouth until we make sure she's inside and safely hidden," added Andrea.

Yep. Madness. Everywhere, madness.

Half dragging the poor woman into my home, Andrea and Pandora placed Valerie in my office. They joined Keisha and me at the breakfast table.

"Are you crazy? What is wrong with all of you? We're going to be arrested!" I cried.

"We're going to be rewarded," said Andrea brightly.

Am I the only sane person left in Sweet Briar? Had something evil seeped into the water, and my love of coffee notwithstanding, I'd managed to elude the effects of it in some way?

"Explain."

"Lorcan called me just now. You were right, Dorie. They're all gone!" said Andrea. Keisha nodded and shot me a look of sympathy.

"Don't stress, Lily. All will be explained shortly. You've been knee-deep in festival duty, not to mention keeping an eye on Adriana, so she doesn't run off half-cocked and get into trouble. And don't you be telling her I said that!"

Keisha had her hands full on her nights watching Antonio while trying to keep an eye on Adriana as well. She looked as exhausted as I felt. I wondered how she managed to do it all and remain so positive.

"Who is 'all gone,' and what does it have to do with kidnapping Valerie?" I asked. "And what was all that about a séance?"

"That was just a diversion attempt. I intended to nab Valerie all along," said Dorie, confounding me beyond all reason.

I moved into the kitchen to check on Wicked's food and water, and it hit me all at once that I'd forgotten I had no need to do so. That's when the floodgates opened, and all the stress of the last few weeks came out in a stream of ugly tears.

Sobbing in my hands, I allowed Andrea to lead me into the den. That's where a brand new set of comfy furniture, provided by a repentant Pandora, waited for me to sink down in comfort and continue with my lachrymose.

"Let it out, Lily. You'll feel better," said Keisha gently.

Andrea rushed over with a mug of coffee, and Pandora

settled in the chair across from me, waiting, if not patiently, at least quietly, while I cried it out.

Finally, I managed to get control of myself and repeated my question. This time a bit more politely.

"Please, won't someone explain?"

And they did.

"Do you mean to tell me everyone we know who's been suffering this malady is now missing?" I cried.

Keisha nodded yes and patted my knee.

"Every single one of them. Dev Patel was the first after your dad and Dennis ran off with Chester behind the wheel and Hester goading him on from the back seat," explained Pandora.

"Followed by Shirley Jones, that nice man who runs the French café, Julia Crawley, Hermione Winters, Lowell Hickinbottom, your dad, Dennis, and the Soules. For all we know, Rusty has abandoned Frank and is out there in the woods baying at the moon," said Dorie.

"Is that everyone? No...Maureen..."

"Is tied up in June's apartment. She's watching her until Jake can arrive and bring her here."

What? Even *Jake* is involved in this mess?

"I mentioned Lorcan just called. He confirmed Jack Borza hadn't shown up for work, and when he called his cell, there was no answer. A call to his parents confirmed they hadn't seen him in a few days. So we assume he's gone too," said Keisha. "Now Lorcan's gone to help Jake get Maureen here safely."

"And Judge Cornelius never returned from that hunting lodge he was supposed to be at. Wilhelmina isn't helping things, and even Boris has now closed ranks. They aren't allowing anyone on the property. It will take a decree from The Order of Origin for those people to allow us entry," Andrea added.

"And here I thought Boris had come to some sense. You said he'd even offered to go retrieve Judge Dietrich. I guess that never happened," said Keisha.

"Maybe I should call Cousin Maggie. After all, she is head of the Order here in the States. No need to contact them overseas," I wondered aloud.

"Jeebers, no! We don't need the Order aware that any of this is going down, Lily. That's the last thing we'd want!" cried Dorie, with Keisha and Andrea nodding in agreement.

OK, then.

"This needs to be done on the quiet...nice and organized. Which is why we're having a bit of a pow-wow tonight. Here. At your place," said Andrea with an apologetic smile.

"Who's coming?"

CLANG!

"Me, for one!" Edith popped into the room and swirled around, looking self-important with her ghost notepad at the ready, a pen tucked behind one ear. "I'm here to take notes!"

She'd barely finished speaking when I heard tires on gravel and the slamming of many car doors. The baying of the hellhounds all but drowned them out.

"Awesome! It appears the party is about to start!" exclaimed Dorie excitedly.

Nice and quiet? Organized? It sounded like the circus had arrived and was setting up shop in my backyard.

How come I expected the worst?

CHAPTER 17

*E*xpect the worst and hope for the best. In my case, it could have been much worse, but the bevy of people who'd arrived bringing food and drink could only help solve this mystery...or die trying.

Aunt Iona and Uncle Owen arrived with Douglas, and much to my continued surprise, had Nora in tow.

Eileen and Henry, Lorcan's parents, arrived with my mother, who looked the worse for wear. I knew not knowing where Charlie had run off to was killing her. And I suspected that because he'd left her behind despite the affliction, hurt more than his running away in the first place.

Lorcan came next with Jake, and they led a sullen Maureen Kennedy into the dining room with June following. Abner was behind them, followed by Aunt Chiara, Uncle Stephen, Steve Junior, and Becky.

Brian Chase showed up next, and his guest rendered me speechless. Rita Chase arrived with her son and sat beside a weeping June. I did not expect that!

The front doorbell rang, and Lorcan rushed to answer it, allowing Sheila entry, her arms laden with bags from Joe's

Diner where she worked. Accompanying her was Stu Jones, our esteemed (not really!) mayor, and Sheila and Shirley's baby brother.

"Gordy couldn't make it but sends his good wishes and hopes for luck tonight," Sheila explained as she began setting trays of food onto the table.

I silently thanked the architect and my great-grandparents' desire for an enormously large family since they were the ones to plan this home's every detail. Yes, my dining room could easily fit thirty people...especially with the additional leaves added to my table and chairs gathered from elsewhere in the home.

Lastly, to my surprise, Grandpa Antonio and Adriana entered the dining room and took a seat at the opposite end of the table facing yours truly.

Well, well...the gang most definitely is all here!

"First we eat, then we talk!" ordered Pandora. No one argued, especially when Uncle Stephen mentioned he'd brought along three ginormous pastry boxes filled with delightful delicacies for dessert.

Despite my anxiety, my mouth drooled in anticipation of the feast in which we were about to take part.

* * *

SOMEWHERE IN THE middle of our dining, it was ascertained both Maureen and Valerie had shown no signs of taking flight. So with some trepidation, both were allowed a seat at the table. I'd never *served* such a crowd before.

Grateful to be freed and having had a satisfactory explanation for why they'd been bound and kidnapped, both women were more apt to forgive and forget—especially since we'd stuffed them full of delicious vittles. However, Valerie appeared rather mutinous and kept shooting dark looks in Pandora's direction.

We'd have to deal with that at a later date.

Maureen, rendered mostly speechless while ogling everyone present, seemed out of place and highly nervous. She kept eyeing my décor and I noticed a wistful mien cross her face. Maureen caught me watching her and blushed, quickly dropping her eyes to her dinner plate.

"Here, Maureen...try a meatball," said my cousin Steve, handing her one. "They're divine."

"Thank you," the poor girl turned fifteen shades of red before taking a tiny nibble of the delectable treat.

Maureen had been carefully avoiding staring directly at Pandora, who'd been trying to engage and making it rather apparent—taunting and intimidation were her favorite pastimes, after all. Case in point, she'd locked eyes on Maureen's face for the last ten minutes while slurping up spaghetti one thin noodle at a time and hadn't blinked once.

"Dorie."

"What?" she smirked but didn't ease up. I think it had to do with the fact Steve dared speak to the girl. I noticed Steve awkwardly avoided engaging, not paying any attention to the crossroads demon. Pandora seemed indifferent, and I summed it up to past lovers and their issues. It was probably a factor in Dorie poking at Maureen, although she enjoyed doing so from the moment they had met.

Edith even got into the action by popping up from the table in front of Maureen, but she couldn't detect her, so it was all for nothing.

"Attention, everyone! Shall we get down to business?" Gloria called everyone to order and began handing out notebooks and pens. My family was big on taking notes and making lists.

"Now...what do we know so far and is anyone not accounted for who's stricken?" she asked.

"Oh!" Nora made a soft exclamation and then passed her notebook over to me. "This must be yours."

When I glanced at it, I too began to blush and quickly turned a few pages to conceal what I'd written down. I'd forgotten I'd started to make wedding plans in earnest. Andrea peered over from her spot next to me, grinned, and winked at Becky, who giggled. Lorcan leaned over and kissed my temple, causing me to melt a little.

"If you two lovebirds can keep your hands off each other for a second, we have pressing issues to deal with here," snapped Adriana.

Despite the seriousness of the situation, I stuck my tongue out and her and blew a raspberry. She just cackled at me and flipped me the bird. Maureen gawked at the interplay. I guessed she wasn't used to such familial dynamics.

Belatedly, I remembered the rumors of verbal abuse in her family and gave her a reassuring smile.

Imagine my surprise when Maureen returned it.

My cousin, Douglas, had too much wine and began blowing raspberries at everyone. "Sláinte!" he cried, jumping up and raising his goblet.

"Sit down, you ninny. You're drunk!" scolded Nora with a nod to her dad to move her brother out into the next room.

Uncle Owen sighed and acquiesced. Just a typical meal with my relations!

"All those who reported hearing voices, except Ms. Parks and Ms. Kennedy, have run off to places unknown," stated Henry.

Eileen wrote down what he'd said and looked up expectantly for him to continue. I was grateful Lorcan's parents had been spared this malady. I didn't know how the empath would react if his own parents should run away from home.

Without Lorcan and his soothing presence, we'd all run amok.

"Do we know of anyone acting strangely...perhaps not allowing for it being due to voices plaguing them?" asked Tanaquil.

"This is a small town, but we can't keep track of everyone. We wouldn't have known about Jack had Lorcan not confronted him for almost forgetting to replace oil in a vehicle he'd serviced. Almost cost the owners money...that would have caused a mess," said Henry, once more doing his part.

"He didn't want anyone knowing...the stigma of folks thinking he might be going crazy," said Lorcan.

"I wonder how many more in this town are hiding the fact?" I asked.

"We could do a wellness check...my officers and me," Brian offered. "It will take some time, but we could get Glen and his people involved, and possibly the fire department and EMT's...combined, we could really cover some ground."

"Here's the question of the hour," said Andrea. "Who is behind the voices? Who is doing this and why?"

"It's a witch," Maureen stated softly.

"Come again?" cried Adriana. "Speak up, young lady. Some of us are hard of hearing."

Since when?

I glared at Adriana, and she flipped me off...*again*.

"I said I think it must be a witch."

"Why do you say that, dear?" asked June, addressing her employee kindly.

"Because I think I recognize the voice...and I'm sure I've figured out how we became infected."

If Maureen wanted the spotlight, she sure knew how to get everyone's undivided attention in a hurry.

This was going to be interesting.

CHAPTER 18

"*I*f it looks like a witch, and acts like a witch...and sounds like a witch, it must be a duck," joked Pandora.

"Quit it, you," I ordered.

"Go ahead and tell us again why you are blaming Hester Soule? I'm not accusing you of anything, Maureen...but Hester?"

Maureen looked like she wanted to cry but squared her shoulders and continued her theory.

"Hear me out. Hester isn't the actual voice speaking in my head. I think those of us who came in contact with her, or more importantly, sampled her pumpkin spice cold brew became infected by it, and the voice took hold."

The room erupted in mumbles as everyone began quietly discussing amongst themselves and Tanaquil had the rap on the table to regain order.

"How do you figure?" asked Jake.

I noted Nora nodding in agreement and appearing satisfied in some way. What was that about?

Maureen cleared her throat and explained. "I was on the Fall Festival's cleanup committee and made lists of the different teams and when they'd be working. Then, this morning, I cleaned my junk drawer and pulled out the paper. I was about to toss it when the names jumped out at me."

Maureen squirmed in her chair and pouted. "I was going to tell June what I'd discovered, but that was when you and Lorcan rushed in and tied me up," she addressed Jake. "Everyone who'd worked on my team that day drank some of Hester's brew. All of us are suffering from the voices in our head."

"Charlie went on and on about that beverage," said Adelaide sadly. "He said it was the best pumpkin drink he'd ever tasted."

"Dennis too," whispered Rita. "He came to my shop asking if I had any spice bend to compete with Hester's." June smiled at Rita sadly, then patted her hand.

"That's right!" cried Valerie. "It was the first time I'd volunteered at anything...I did drink some of it. But I only took a sip."

"Me too," said Maureen. "I don't really like pumpkin...I was only being polite."

Well, that certainly could be one reason they both hadn't run off when summoned. Valerie and Maureen could now resist the voice, it seemed. So it had to be Hester's potion. But why would she do something like this?

"Hang on a minute. Back up. That doesn't add up concerning Shirley," I said. "Sure, she was there and had more than a sip of Hester's drink, but that doesn't explain why she's been hearing voices since February."

There were loud exclamations of surprise since most of my guests weren't privy to that fact.

"That means Hester drank some of her own concoction and is suffering this malady as well...or a diabolical mastermind plotting some kind of nefarious evil," said Uncle Owen. "As for Shirley, maybe the voice she heard in February isn't the same one as who everyone is hearing now. But Hester? How can that woman be evil? Oh, I don't know!" Owen began rubbing his head.

That was a sobering thought. Hester might be a pint-sized nuisance with her measuring tape, trying to size you up for your own coffin—but never a casket—and could creep you out just as much as her brother, Chester, but I didn't want her to be a baddie.

I felt it my dark witch duty to take out the baddies who came for my town and loved ones.

"Teeth, Lily. Settle down," murmured Adelaide, pointing to my face.

I assumed my eyes had darkened, felt my teeth dipping down, and forced myself to take a few calming breaths.

Maureen's eyes widened, and I thought she might pass out. That's right. She's never seen me go all goth. Nora too, seemed disturbed by the sight. Which made it all the more amazing when she opened her mouth to add her input.

"I think we must send Lily back onto the Dietrich estate."

All eyes turned to my cousin.

"I'm sure Edith is here and can explain. But let me try. You see…Hester isn't one to make spiced beverages or any kind of offerings when volunteering. She usually likes to be on the sewing crew. So why suddenly make a draught of anything?"

Adriana rubbed her chin deep in thought. Then, snapping her fingers at Sheila, my grandmother barked a question, "You told me about that incident the day after it happened when I came into the diner. So, you were there. What did you see?"

Nora clammed up and crossed her arms, obviously hurt that Adriana dismissed her so effortlessly.

Sheila considered her words carefully, trying to recall the occurrence. "You know...now that I think about it, Shirley and I were there that day. She was volunteering, and I stopped by on my way to work to see her."

Sheila tapped her fingers on the table and frowned. "Wait a minute. Shirley said something about Wilhelmina Dietrich. Let me think. I know! She said Willie asked Hester if she still had more of the 'special mix' left over."

"What special mix?" I cried.

"That's what I was trying to tell you," said Nora, flashing a heated look in Adriana's direction. "Wilhelmina and Boris have this greenhouse where they grow all sorts of exotic herbs and spices. They claim they have a mix that eases migraines and allows for deep sleep. Hester blushed and said she might have used some of it to make her pumpkin brew!"

Really? And *now* Nora thought to tell us?

"Why are you still hanging around that insufferable family anyway?" asked Aunt Iona, frowning at her daughter.

"I do it for Edith. I feel close to her there," whispered Nora, looking down at her hands. "Plus...well, I'm spying on them in a way. To help our family."

Unbeknownst to her, Edith—all dewy-eyed and sniffling —swooshed over to Nora's side and wrapped her arms around her old friend. Nora even shivered a little but made no comment. Finally, Nora met my eyes, and I smiled in understanding and she smiled back.

I caught movement on my left and noticed Aunt Iona dabbing her eyes with a tissue.

"Perhaps Wilhelmina has jar upon jar of the mix, and she somehow shared it with my sister. I mean, I can't imagine why Shirley would take anything that vile woman handed out, but you never know," said Sheila, all the while wringing her hands.

"There is no doubt that Wilhelmina is behind this...not

Hester. She's just a pawn. That's why Lily needs to sneak back onto the estate and get proof. The greenhouse holds the answers, and we need to discover what else that woman is up to," said Nora.

"It's not what's in the greenhouse. It's what's in our old oak tree," said Edith, not that many could hear her. But I did...and so did Adriana and Dorie.

"What is this? What tree?" asked Adriana.

"Edith's family has this weird old oak tree. I saw it myself the other night."

Nora's eyes grew large and round. "Is Edith here?"

I nodded yes and pointed to the spot just over her left shoulder. Sometimes Edith could be seen by more than just me, Adriana, and Pandora. Other times, only her voice came through...or a brief glance. I think it had something to do with her energy output and the acceptance of those needing to see her. But right now, the group was at a disadvantage.

Then I did something no one expected, but a few had witnessed before...I cast a dark reveal spell on my notebook. Then, sliding it over to Edith's side of the table, I ignored how just about everyone present cringed and cowered as I did so.

Edith, however, knew what to do and began to speak again.

Only this time, her words appeared in perfect cursive across the book's pages.

"There is a hidden entrance in the oak tree near the greenhouse. Inside is a laboratory where highly controversial magic is imbued into ordinary herbs and spices. If I had more details of this situation, I might have accused my family...definitely my grandmother."

Everyone remained transfixed on the writing, and Edith continued.

"There is something more disturbing we need to address,

however. There is only one other person alive I know of who knows of this lab and has been inside gathering ingredients for her aunt to use in a retail setting," said Edith.

"Rowan Nightingale," cried Maureen. "It's her voice I hear in my head!"

CHAPTER 19

"We need to be smart about this and not make any mistakes."

I turned to face Adriana and Andrea in the backseat while Dorie rode shotgun up front again. Alas, Keisha couldn't rejoin our little group, it being her night to watch Antonio. But this time, we had Edith agreeing to show up and help us get in that tree—without any fanfare on her part. The last thing we needed was clanging bells heralding her arrival.

Who knew the Dietrichs, Langsfords, and Planks had a magic oak tree in their yard? We didn't have anything like that.

I think.

"We need to not get caught this time," grumbled Andrea, holding up her invisibility cloak.

"More importantly, we need to get evidence to take down that beastly woman once and for all, but not tip her off that we've discovered her laboratory nor gathered any proof. This needs to be a clean B&E and fact-finding mission...along with the confiscation of just a sample of items," stated Adriana. "Hopefully, Spooky can get us in the tree."

"Don't antagonize Edith when we get there. This is her family, after all," I grumbled.

"I say we blow it all up," cried Dorie. "What? Don't pretend you wouldn't like to see the place blow sky high with Willie riding a rocket into space."

Well, yeah, but we are licensed professionals now. I deputized my riding companions as part of my High Investigator status. I just hoped I had the authority to do so.

"We definitely need evidence, and then we need to high-tail it out of there and proceed to step two," I said.

"What is step two?" asked Andrea.

"Discovering where the missing are and seeing if Rowan Nightingale is with them...or worse."

"It *better* not be anything worse, or that little witch is toast," said Adriana with clenched teeth.

"Rowan is toast anyway," stated Dorie with an evil chuckle, "only she has no idea yet."

I drove almost to the estate, but this time instead of parking near the woods and sneaking onto the property from the right and having to run across that vast expanse of lawn, we decided to approach from the west, on the left side of the property. But this had its disadvantages.

"I can't believe we must walk through a marsh," complained Andrea.

"It's not a marsh, Whiny Britches. Those wetlands are buried in a forest setting, otherwise known as a swamp," drawled Adriana.

"And that makes it better?" asked Andrea miserably. "Either way, we will still get wet. And I'm not a Whiny Britches."

"Are too."

"Am not!"

"Are too, Whiny. And I have no intention of getting wet," stated Adriana.

It was rather funny hearing someone else go back and forth with the old battleax, but even I knew to defend Andrea and query how we'd manage to not get wet.

"But...it's a swamp. How do we remain dry?" I asked.

"Duh. Really you two! We use magic!" barked Adriana, rolling her eyes so violently I reached out and grappled a small sapling tree in case the ground shifted under our feet.

Magic. Yes...that makes sense. However...

"Won't that draw attention to us...or weaken us slightly?" I asked.

"Liliana. The minuscule energy expended to keep us dry won't matter in the grand scheme of things. And is certainly better than the alternative."

"The alternative?"

"Having to plod through dank, slimy water and get bit by water moccasins and sucked on by leeches."

There is that.

* * *

AND HERE I thought Adriana had a spell that would cause us to float across the terrain, landing safely—and very much dry —at the western gates of the Dietrich/Langsford estate.

But no.

"Really? Waders? That's your magic trick, old woman?" I asked, disappointment clouding my voice.

"Hey! They're made out of vulcanized rubber," argued Adriana.

"But...any fisherman can wear these and get around. This isn't magic!" said Andrea, staring dismally at the dark moss green fishing gear.

"Oh, really, Smarty Pants? And do regular old fishermen look like this?" with a flourish of waving hands, blue sparks flowing from her fingertips, Adriana did something to the water apparel so it wrapped around each of us until we'd morphed into Cat Woman—er, Women—but without the masks.

Seriously, our body wet suits were so formfitting they didn't leave much to the imagination as far as the shape or nuance of our bodies was concerned.

"What happened to our clothes?" I mewed, distraught.

"Magic," replied Adriana smugly.

"No, seriously. I want something to act as a barrier between this stuff...it...it feels like a second skin!" I cried.

"That's because it is," said Dorie in consternation. But then she gazed at herself and smiled. "Damn. I look good!"

"My butt looks huge in this getup!" cried Andrea.

"That's because..."

"Shut it, you old bat. No body shaming!" I cried.

"I was going to say it's because Andrea is short for her weight," replied Adriana primly.

"I'm going on a diet," wailed Andrea.

"Fat chance of that working, considering she's in a bakery all day," whispered Adriana. Loudly.

"I heard that!"

"You were meant to. Now come along!"

WE'D SLOSHED our way across the primarily dry swamp, only plunging to chest level once. The rest of the time, we were on muddy land with the occasional foray into the knee-deep green water. The only deterrent was the copious number of gnats and mosquitos, which buzzed and whined around our heads. Unfortunately, we spent more time slapping them away than watching where we were going.

Thankfully, no one wound up face down in the muck and mire.

It took us forty minutes, but we'd finally arrived at the fence.

"Now what?" asked Andrea.

"Now we wait for Edith's signal and..."

"Would that be it?" Dorie pointed at the gnarled oak, which now resembled a living entity. No...seriously. The tree had flaming red eyes and was staring at us menacingly.

"Hey! Is that...it IS! Look, Wicked is back! How did she escape the Lincoln?" I was so overjoyed at spying my beloved feline hunched at the base of the tree I hadn't noticed Edith appear by my side.

"Seriously? Have we not seen your cat practically on her own driving your Jeep down Main Street?" said Adriana.

She had a point.

"Quick, you need to climb the fence and...whoa! What are you people wearing?" Edith was agog, taking in the ensemble and what we were wearing. "You look like obscene deep sea divers. Do you realize I can see every wrinkle and fold on your..."

"Edith! Can you please keep on track? What must we do to get into that tree?" I asked, forestalling any further comment about how well we fit our second skin. "And why can't we have our clothing back now?"

This I addressed to Adriana.

"No time."

"Seriously? I need my phone...and pockets. I brought supplies, gloves...you know, stuff!" I argued.

Resigned, Adriana waved her hand again, and our clothing returned, a pile of normal-looking waders heaped at our feet.

I turned to gaze at the fence. Without Keisha and her incredible bag full of tools, I made to climb the barrier but got yanked back by Pandora before I could reach it.

"What?" I asked.

"Warded. Think, silly. I'm sure Willie made sure the perimeter of her property is heavily warded," said Pandora.

"Sorry, yes...of course! I wasn't thinking fully. I make a lousy Head Investigator, don't I?" I replied glumly.

"Don't you dare have a pity party, Liliana. You are new to all this magic. Even though you've been with us a while now. It doesn't come naturally to you. However, sticking your nose into everyone's business and uncovering secrets is right up your alley."

Thanks, I think?

"How do we get over then?" asked Andrea scratching her elbow again.

"I've got this," said Dorie.

One minute we were standing on one side of the fence, but the next, we were transported to the other by some kind of demon magic Pandora had up her sleeve, or...er...body suit.

"If you could have done that, why did we have to walk all the way through that marsh!" Andrea whispered furiously now that we were close to the mansion.

"Too much magic. Anyone paranormal in one square mile would have sensed it. This was more a mental exercise for me and hardly took anything arcane."

Yeah, well, it felt like I'd swam through a river of ice and fire. My skin is still itchy and tingled from the experience.

We hurried over to the tree and awaited instruction.

"Stop right there!" said Edith. "Any further, and you'll trigger the Sentinels."

We froze in place and watched in horror as Wicked trotted over to us and began weaving in and around my ankles.

"Calm down! She's too small to set off the alarm. Now, listen carefully. Lily, you must pick up one or two of those rocks at your feet and hit the tree right in the eyes. I already opened the first lock by chanting the spell which triggers the tree to open its eyes."

"A tree can have eyes?" I wondered.

"This one does. It's a magical tree."

No, really?

Be nice! I jumped at the familiar sound of Wicked speaking to me and looked down at her lazily blinking up at me.

"Glad the tree could still hear you since you're in ghost form," said Andrea, peering around the yard watching for Sentinels...or Wilhelmina and her wand.

Noticing several piles of smooth rounded stones littering the lawn, I could see how tossing them accurately and hitting the eyes were part of the entry process. Anyone who happened by would more than likely get smushed to a pancake by the Sentinels and never figure out the rock puzzle...nor know the spell to get the tree to open its eyes in the first place.

Genius security measures!

"Will it only work with your voice and that of your family?" I asked.

"You'd think they would have thought of everything little failsafe, but no. Rowan used to come down here to gather herbs when Samantha needed them for Rita's shop. It's one of the reasons Nora and I recruited her for...um...our other activities. We saw so much of her."

Edith was obviously speaking of her drug-selling teens and their side business. It started her down the path to her end days. Only she surprised everyone by remaining behind as a ghost and was now on our side.

"Well, there's no time like the present to see how good of an aim I have!" I said, changing the subject and bringing Edith out of such maudlin thoughts.

Hefting two of the small stones in my hand, I tried to gauge the distance, speed, and other terms I thought I needed for physics and mathematics to work. Then I sent the missile flying through the air and watched as it missed the tree entirely.

"Here, let me." Adriana picked up two stones and squinted her eyes, tongue poking out one side of her mouth, then hurled them toward the tree.

She missed the tree and hit Andrea instead.

"Ow!"

"Hush!"

"But she hit me!" whimpered my cousin, who now switched from scratching her elbow to rubbing it.

"Try again, Lily," said Pandora.

I did as instructed, this time managing to hit the tree but not my target. How frustrating!

"This is getting us nowhere," grumbled Adriana.

"Here, let me give it a whirl." Pandora stood beside me, gathering her own stones, and barely positioned herself before sending them torpedoing toward the tree...and nailed both eyes simultaneously!

"Holy...did you *see* that?" squeaked Andrea.

Rushing over to its base, we again placed our hands on the bark, but the tree remained cool this time.

"So how do we get inside of it? Last time it was as hot as embers when we...gah!"

One minute I was upright and rubbing my hand across the wizened wood. The next, I found myself pitching forward and tumbling downward like some demented Alice falling into the rabbit hole. I didn't go far, realizing I was on a precipice, a smallish edge that gave me the perfect view of a bottomless pit far below. I felt Wicked coil around my ankles, so I knew she'd followed, and I could hear Adriana and Dorie gather behind me even as Andrea, flipping head over heels, passed us, careening into the darkness beyond.

"All that extra padding does wonders for velocity," cackled Adriana mercilessly.

CHAPTER 20

e followed a staircase downward as instructed by Edith until we reached the bottom, and Andrea rubbed her behind and moaned in misery. Adriana had conjured a bouncing ball of light which gave us just enough of a glow to see a few feet ahead.

"Someone could have warned us," she said, glaring at nothing, but the intent was for Edith, who shrugged at me and giggled.

"I heard that, Edith Plank!"

Sobering, Edith led us to an old green door. "Beyond here is the laboratory where the dried herbs and spices are kept."

"Any booby traps to worry about?" I asked.

"No. Why would there be?" replied Edith.

Why indeed? I guess anyone who'd reached this far was supposed to be here.

Moving beyond the entry area, we soon gathered in the laboratory, and Edith directed me to where the light switch dangled. It was an old-fashioned pull string, and I gave it a gentle tug which flooded the space with a soft light. Donning cotton gloves, we got to work.

"Wow. Look at this place!" Andrea scampered around, opening and closing drawers, while Adriana took stock of the ingredients hanging from rafters.

I pulled out my phone and began a systematic search, cataloging each item, and making special notes of the things Pandora and Adriana suggested might get Wilhelmina in trouble for having. I found notes on illegal herbs and recipes for using them that curdled my blood. Snapping away, I noted the handwriting appeared to be Wilhelmina's—I'd certainly seen it enough times on decrees, and formal accusations served to me at one time or another.

That completed, I turned and wandered over to a large desk and began rummaging through each drawer. It didn't take long for me to find something more incriminating than the recipes. Again, in Wilhelmina's precise cursive, I found a list of names—most all of them related to me in one way or another —and plans on how and when to eliminate them one by one.

A name circled in red several times was none other than yours truly. I snapped away and then signaled to Adriana, who came over to see what I'd discovered.

Wicked jumped up on the top of the desk and began knocking items onto the floor. Cats!

"Let's hope Willie has a jar marked 'special mix,' and we aren't in a needle in a haystack situation here," said Adriana. "This is enough damage to get Willie in deep trouble, but I want a direct link between her mix and its role in making folks hear Rowan in their minds."

"If we are to believe Maureen," I stated halfheartedly. After all, I didn't detect any deception behind her story.

"What is this board over here," asked Andrea, indicating a large rectangle hanging on the wall with wires and buttons, of which several were lit up.

"That's our old intercom system, and whatever you do, do

not push one of those buttons, or we'll be discovered," said Edith. I had to relay this message to Andrea, who gave us a thumbs-up.

I chased Wicked away from the desk and opened the last drawer.

"I can't believe it! Look!" Holding up a small Tupperware container, I pointed to what was written on the masking tape label across the top.

"Special mix. Wow. How dumb do you have to be?" asked Adriana to no one in particular.

I opened the lid and put a large sample in a plastic bag I'd tucked in my pocket. I looked at my great-grandmother as if to say, 'See, I needed my pockets!'

"What about those levers on the wall," asked Dorie, not interested in our search despite the fact we now had proof.

"Oh...those open areas to other rooms. Passageways, if you will, that lead to the well room, the dungeon, and the house beyond."

"Dungeon?" Pandora hit us with a rictus grin, rubbing her hands together. Then, before you could say, 'stop!' she was off and running. Pulling all the levers at once, Dorie tore through a door we'd not noticed it was so covered with layer upon layer of moss.

"Dorie!" I hissed furiously to deaf ears. "I'm going to pummel that demon."

My party gave chase, which was easy to do since Dorie had her own bouncing ball of light to help lead her down the twisted and winding corridor. Edith flashed ahead and berated the imp to no avail.

It came as a surprise to me that I had no need for light. Vampire's eyes. Who knew my latent vampire abilities would come in handy? I surely didn't give it any thought, and now I knew I'd need someone—perhaps Mortimer or Caliente, his girlfriend—to provide me with insight on all things to do with bloodsuckers.

We dared not call out to Pandora, not knowing where this path led. We could be directly under the house for all we knew, and with a sketchy, aged intercom system, who knew how the sound would travel?

I was worried about Adriana keeping up, but my granny was wily and quick. It was Andrea who fell behind, barely managing to stay in sight. She waved us on and did her best to follow. Wicked had streaked by me and now kept pace with the crossroads demon.

After what seemed like five minutes of tortuous exercise, we screeched to a halt in a circular room that held several passages leading to parts unknown. I shouldn't say unknown because tiny wooden signs were pointing the way. Like a bullet shot out of a gun, Dorie took the path leading to the dungeon.

We followed because what choice did we have? At this point, even I was curious. Realizing we'd stopped giving chase and had joined her in this insanity, Pandora slowed the pace, which allowed Andrea to catch up to us, and Adriana to not strain herself.

Finally, we found an old iron door partially open due to Dorie flipping all the levers back in the lab.

"I'm going on a diet," murmured Andrea with a quiet groan.

"If my knee aches tomorrow because of this little junket, it will be you rubbing joint cream on my body, Pandora," warned Adriana in a hushed voice.

"Is someone there? Boris? Arthur? Stella...is that you? Somebody...please."

Our mouths dropped open as we ogled one another, not daring to breathe. That sounded like Cornelius! My stellar vampiric ability to scent things hadn't detected any living being in the dungeon when we'd passed outside...unless Cornelius was a recent addition to its chamber.

Adriana shrugged and made to open the door wide when Edith stopped her.

"It creaks something awful. Look...it's open enough so you can slip around it. Let's not advertise we're here," she said.

We did just that, slinking around the entrance and coming to stand before a wide-eyed and very bound Judge Dietrich. The man looked a mess, all rumbled and bedraggled, his silver hair standing askew. He even had dirt smudges and heaven knew what else on his face and clothing.

"Corny! What on earth happened here?" asked Adriana quietly.

"It's Wilhelmina, Annie. She's gone completely insane."

Now you think that? I could have told you ages ago your sister was a cracked nut, mister.

"Is it because she lied about you hearing voices?" I asked. Wondering if that were the reason.

"No. I hear, well...heard them. It's fading now. But I distinctly heard a voice calling to me," he replied.

"Let me guess. You're going to claim Liliana is behind this, and her voice has taunted you for weeks," Adriana accused the man, who shook his head no and appeared shocked at the charge.

"Accuse Lily? Why would I say something to that effect?"

"Because that's what Wille has been spouting all over town! It forced my great-granddaughter to appear before Tanaquil and Olivia with these trumped-up charges!"

"My sister needs help," sighed Cornelius. "I'm sorry this is happening. She's kept virtually everyone in our family hostage with her demented ravings and schemes for months.

And now? As you can see, she has imprisoned me for threatening to report my discovery to the authorities."

Edith looked chagrined and placed her arms around her great-uncle. I watched goosebumps appear on his arms, but he didn't react, not knowing his great-niece was close.

"You know who is behind this," I stated.

"I do."

Not wanting Maureen's claims to be valid, I nonetheless needed to hear it from Judge Dietrich's own mouth before I genuinely believed it a fact.

"I'm sorry, Lily, but I recognized that young lady who is such a thorn in the side of both your family and mine. It's Rowan Nightingale I'm hearing."

Fudge biscuits.

"What do we do now?"

Now we head out to find Rowan and her victims. They're nearby.

"Apparently, our loved ones are close," I informed my group.

"How do you know this?" asked Adriana.

I cocked my thumb in Wicked's direction with a smug I-told-you-so look on my face.

"That cat can speak?" asked the judge incredulously. "I didn't hear a thing. Why...I never!"

"Never is a long time, Corny. Wicked is one in a million, that's for sure. If Liliana says she can hear the little furball, I believe her!" said Adriana in a vote of confidence.

Pandora and Andrea freed the judge and helped him to his feet. Once we returned the way we had come and entered the laboratory, Cornelius all but exploded in rage when we showed him the evidence of Wilhelmina's wrongdoing.

While everyone gathered more of the remaining evidence with Judge Cornelius's permission, Wicked came and sat by my feet. Looking up, I could hear her telepathically and snorted, considering it was the very thing Rowan had been doing with the help of that mix.

There is only one person Rowan covets, Lily. And she has him now. The others were subterfuge to throw everyone off.

Charlie. My dad. She wants Charlie...has Charlie. I relayed back, and Wicked blinked slowly, which I took as a resounding yes.

Where are they? I asked.

In the tower. Edith's old playhouse.

"Hurry. Rowan took them to the playhouse in the back of the property. Wicked just informed me!" I cried.

"How are we going to do this? Where is Wilhelmina, and what is her role in all this? And the rest of my family...are they guilty as well?" asked the judge. Cornelius may love his family, but he was a man of the law, and I suspected he would come down hard on anyone breaking it—including his kin.

"If they are all involved, we are outnumbered. We need more help!" I began worrying my bottom lip until I felt a hand on my arm.

"Liliana. With you here, we have all the help needed. You, me, Pandora, Andrea. We make quite the team," Adriana smiled. "And Wicked, of course."

Could Adriana be correct? Am I strong enough to take on not only Wilhelmina et al...but Rowan Nightingale and her unknown powers? That tilty-headed teen has been a thorn in the side of all of Sweet Briar...but now? This was personal.

"Be on guard," stated Judge Dietrich. "Let's go up through the house and out the back to the playhouse, so we can see my family's status along the way. And if they raise a hand to stop us, we fight."

I liked our odds a bit more after hearing that. But just a bit.

CHAPTER 21

$\mathcal{W}$ ith Judge Dietrich leading the way, we crept up a vast staircase at the end of one of the passages and made it to the mansion's main floor. No one was stirring...although I did see a mouse and convinced Wicked with a mental command to not give chase.

Party pooper.

Yeah, yeah.

We'd gone through the mudroom into the kitchen, then into the family room, where Cornelius stopped short, crying out. "Boris! Heavens! Stella...Arthur, what happened here?"

Sitting on the sofa, all in a row, were Stella and Arthur Plank and Wilhelmina's husband, Boris. All were wide-eyed and bound but good. Their feet were tied together, and each had tape across their mouths. I guessed their hands were bound behind their backs from how they sat.

Gently removing the tape from Stella's mouth first, Cornelius repeated his question.

"It's mother. She's gone mad!" wailed Stella. Grateful the tape was gone, she nonetheless became shocked when she spied my party. "What are they doing here?"

"Saving your ass," exclaimed the judge. He suddenly gripped his heart and grimaced.

"Corny! Here...sit down and rest. You're dehydrated as it is. Let me get you some water, and then you can finish freeing your family. We've got this other matter," offered Adriana.

Pandora backtracked to the kitchen with Andrea, and they returned with the water and a bowl of chocolate kisses. I guess they figured the sugar would help.

Andrea had scissors and began cutting through the tethers.

Judge Dietrich took a long drink but waved off the treats. "Wilhelmina is my kin."

"And the rest of your family needs you here. So let us tackle this mess," said Adriana gently. Edith morphed into the room, looking more robust than I'd ever seen her.

"I'm here. Mom...Dad. Let me. I can keep an eye on them all."

"Edith! Oh, my little girl! I can see you!" sobbed Stella, Arthur desperately trying to lunge in his daughter's direction.

One glance told me everyone in her family could now see and hear Edith, and I knew they were in good hands. But, at the same time, we moved on to the more serious matter— destroying Wilhelmina and Rowan's reprehensible plans, whatever they may be.

"Andrea. Can you stay here and guard against any surprises? Judge Dietrich is too weary, and I'm afraid so are the rest of them," I asked.

Andrea nodded but threw me her invisibility cloak. "Here, you might need it."

We crept out of the family room, out the back door, and began walking toward the old playhouse.

"Here we go," mumbled Dorie popping a chocolate kiss into her mouth. "What? I'm fortifying myself."

We reached the playhouse without incident but found three unexpected allies waiting for us outside the front door. Adelaide with Nora had grins on their faces and a meek but determined Maureen waited beside them. They were dressed in fighting gear. I supposed my mom outfitted my cousin and Maureen, noting they had a matching ensemble.

"Did you expect me to sit home and gnash my teeth?" Adelaide mumbled softly. "That's my husband that wretched child has in there. I'm going to rattle her cage until she really goes mental."

Pointing to her two companions, my mom continued. "Nora and Maureen figured it out. Nora knew about the playhouse, of course, and Maureen used to come here regularly before...um..."

"Yeah, we get it. The past is in the past, however. Let's get this show on the road," whispered Adriana. "Follow my lead."

"No...allow me. I know my way around in there, and it makes sense I should take us through to where I suspect they must be," said Nora.

What's with this family? I stood staring up at the structure in awe. The "playhouse" was the size of an average suburban house...complete with its own Rapunzel tower. No wonder the local teens used to party here. Heck, I almost wished I could have joined them myself.

Almost.

"Let's roll!" said Dorie.

We all stopped to stare at her.

"What?" she asked. "Too much?"

* * *

WE WOULD BE SORELY DISAPPOINTED if we thought our arrival would go unnoticed. In fact, from the moment we crossed the threshold, we could feel the evil magic pulsing throughout the house. My inner alarm went on such high alert. I could feel my fangs punch out and, for once, didn't care.

Instantly, upon my vampiric abilities taking hold, I felt a calm settle over me.

I could do this.

Still, I took a moment to consider, meditate, and allow my dark witch to regain control. I still had Andrea's cloak in my hands and looked around for somewhere to set it. Maureen reached out. I gave it to her gratefully, then placed my fingers on my temple.

I didn't need to tip my hand so early in the game. My dark witch ability was good enough; I'd save the vamp stuff if and when I needed it later. In and out, I slowly breathed and visualized my intent. Satisfaction coursed through me when I felt my fangs retract and my vision return to normal. I'm getting good at this!

I positioned myself behind Nora, and we began our ascent once we reached the tower's base.

Five steps from the top, I sensed Rowan's presence. The air was heavily scented with some mystery herbs, but this close, I could smell the blood in her veins as well as that of others. I'm not sure how I knew it was Rowan, but then her girlish, tittering laughter reached my ears, and I realized I'd gotten it right.

"Come in, come in. Won't you make yourselves at home?"

"Rowan. How horrible to see you again," I said, my eyes never leaving hers, yet noting the only other person in the room was Wilhelmina. And she looked odd.

"Oh, don't mind Willie. She's been poisoned."

Rowan said this so matter-of-factly it sent a chill down my spine.

"I don't need her anymore, you see."

Pulling a wand from inside her cloak, Rowan sent a stream of magic in Wilhelmina's direction, and the older woman moaned, unable to scream from the stitches that sealed her mouth shut. Instead, tears poured from her eyes, and she seemed to implore us.

"That's a handy little trick, dear. Why don't you show us how you did it by reversing it?" suggested Adriana. I noted she too, had her wand at the ready.

"Oh, no. I couldn't do that, ma'am. Willie is the only one left who knows how to control me. And I refuse to allow that to ever happen to me again. Why...coming to the psych ward, paying me little visits, and watching me like I was a freak to be examined. I never forgot that—or her experiments on my mind."

What's this? Could it be Wilhelmina hadn't been collaborating with Rowan? But the spice mix? The entire travesty with my family and friends. And where are they anyway?

"Child. You do not need to seek revenge. The clerics at the hospital were only trying to help you..."

"Help me? Don't you realize it was Winnie who paid for my treatment? Saving my mother the expense? Oh! Hello, Miss Nora. It's so nice to see you again. I hope I didn't harm you with my magic, but I grew tired of your demands. So you're going to have to die now as well," Rowan tittered, tilting her head to one side. Her laugh was so freakishly annoying.

Tilty-head snotty brat. I thought to myself, grinding my teeth together and scowling.

Rowan surveyed my party, her eyes landing on my mother. "You. You're not getting him back, you know."

"Oh, but I am," said my mother, her voice soft as silk and deadly calm.

"Miss Adriana, I hope you don't mind. I instructed Donna to create that portal that sucked Mr. Antonio into the prison. I heard it aged him greatly." Now outright laughing maniacally, I don't think anyone in the room wanted Rowan to walk out of there alive. Glancing back at my mother, Rowan returned to the previous conversation.

"We shall see about that. I have a feeling you will be disappointed. And who are you?" This Rowan addressed to Pandora. This schizophrenic questioning was making my head hurt.

"A friend of a friend. Hey, I have a question for you. If you could give up your soul and get your heart's desire, would you do it?" asked Dorie nonchalantly.

"I have no soul," replied Rowan darkly.

"But I think you do. So...would you? Give it up?"

"Sure! I mean, like if I can have everything here on earth and my plans go the way I want. So, why not?" laughed the demented twit.

"What do you mean, 'plans.' What are your intentions?" asked Adriana.

Rowan looked each of us in the eye, then twisted her wrist, causing Wilhelmina to whimper and pass out. She fell to the ground with a resounding crash.

Then all hell broke loose.

CHAPTER 22

hey're in a back bedroom!

Wicked's voice came in loud and clear while I ducked from another bolt of magic which landed far closer than I would have preferred. Then, tossing up a forcefield of some sort, Pandora gave us time to reciprocate. Only Rowan had forcefields of her own.

Our magic bounced away, useless.

I relayed that information to Nora, and she crept from the room to go free those imprisoned. That left me, Pandora, and Adriana to battle this lunatic. I didn't know what had happened to Maureen. I assumed she'd taken off once things got nasty. I couldn't blame the kid.

"We need to get Wilhelmina out of here. She's a pawn in this game. We don't know how much was forced on her and how much she did willingly, but I'll not see her harmed before she can see a trial—and help send this whack-job away for life if we don't kill her first," mumbled Adriana as we huddled under the shield.

"I'm not going to be able to hold this much longer. Can

you guys hurry it along here?" whined Dorie as she flicked a steady stream of bolts in Rowan's direction.

"How can she be so strong? I don't understand it," said Adelaide. "She shouldn't be this powerful...and now look at that! She's shimmering."

It only lasted a few seconds, but we all saw Rowan flicker and shimmer before appearing solid again. That was odd.

Rowan frowned but didn't break down her shields. She began inching her way toward Wilhelmina, and I knew we had to do something quickly.

But that's when we heard a scream downstairs, and our blood ran cold.

They are under Rowan's glamour. Nora released everyone from being tied up...then they overwhelmed her! Watch out! There's a back staircase, and they're heading your way!

Wicked's warning came just in time, and I could relay it to my party. I just hoped Nora was alright and nothing deadly had occurred.

Sudden movement across the room signaled the arrival of our missing loved ones. Only now, they were acting like crazed zombies. Zombies holding wands and staring right at us. What was worse, Pandora's shield only covered a small area protecting us from Rowan. But against that hoard, we were not only vulnerable...we were exposed to whatever magic they were about to unleash.

I locked eyes with Pandora and somehow understood what she was about to do. In one quick flash, she propelled herself up and over her own forcefield, then turned and used it to protect us from the zombie kin and them from coming to any harm Rowan might toss their way.

Distract us, then injure the innocent...not on *our* watch!

That worked, but now we had no choice but to go postal on the giggling menace.

Spell after spell, deflection, and wards...on and on we battled. The sweat from exertion was blinding me, and I knew Adriana was fading fast. Adelaide, distracted by the sight of Charlie, had to find inner resolve and focus. She managed to do so, but I knew she was a weak link in our wall of witchy retribution.

Pandora could do nothing but hold that shield, but for how long?

Seemingly with minimal effort, Rowan managed to best us and was growing stronger. But how? I mean...there she was, squatting on the ground near Willie, flicking her wrist and causing so much destruction. Could she be...?

"She's using Willie's magic to bolster herself!"

Wilhelmina looked about spent. Her eyes rolled back into her head, the whites showing, and she'd turned a sickly blue color. "She's killing her!" I screamed.

A dark figure loomed behind Pandora, and I heard my mother's intake of breath. Daring a glance in that direction, I witnessed my dad performing some kind of magic that looked to be working through the shield—and heading directly toward Dorie's head.

Adelaide jumped up and ran toward them both. "Charlie, no!"

Rowan smiled and moved her right hand in a circular pattern, and I watched as a sickly black orb formed above it. Hundreds of tiny spiders were coiled into a ball of energy that flickered and pulsed, ready to fly across the room. She flicked her eyes over to Adelaide, then back to me, and bared her teeth. "Say goodbye to Mama!"

Rowan hefted the ball of energy like a baseball she was preparing to pitch, and I stood growling in her direction.

"You are not going to do this evil. Not now, not ever, Rowan Nightingale."

Now was the time for surprises, and I willed my vampiric side to come out and play. I knew I had unnerved Rowan when the ball shrunk in size, and she almost dropped it.

"What is this? You're not a vampire. It's only an illusion!"

I felt my eyes go black, and it was my turn to chuckle wickedly. "I'm no illusion."

Preparing to flash and end this threat, I didn't expect Rowan to have one last card up her sleeve. Opening her mouth, I flinched as a dark, inky liquid began to coil and ooze from it. Rowan herself began to fade, but the miasma snaked around the room and then ricocheted over to the window, where it flung itself out to the safety beyond.

I could hear my mom struggling behind me, crying out even as Charlie roared in some kind of pain and anger.

Rowan managed a weak smile before doing one last thing before fading completely. Hurling the ball in the direction of my parents, she gave me a wink before watching her magic slam into them.

"No!" I screamed in horror and watched as the black ball flew through the air. But instead of hitting Adelaide and Charlie, it slammed into Maureen Kennedy, who'd just materialized from under Andrea's invisibility cloak, taking the full brunt of the vile magic and saving my parents.

It was Rowan's turn to yell, only she faded out with a popping sound before her raging screams could be heard.

It was over that quick, only we knew nothing would ever be the same again.

With the magic gone, and the inky presence which resided in Rowan gone along with it, all our loved ones instantly snapped out of their funk. Charlie crashed into Adelaide, swooping her up and showering her with kisses and apologies.

"I've let you down again. Oh, my love, I'm so sorry!"

sobbing and broken, Charlie Sweet crumbled to the ground, dragging my mother along with him.

"It will be OK, darling. We will get past this just like always. I'm here. I'll always be here."

But the haunted expression on my father's face belied the fact his mind, so recently stitched together by love, was once again splintered by the darkest of evil. And I vowed to end it or die trying.

Wicked entered the room, ran over to my parents, and promptly climbed onto Charlie's lap. My dad curled his fingers in her soft fur and began to sob.

No. Things would never be the same again.

I stumbled over to where Maureen had fallen and looked down at her broken body.

"She sacrificed herself for my parents," I whispered as Pandora sidled beside me. I felt a tightness in my chest and didn't realize I was crying until Dorie wrapped me up in a hug and let me cry it out.

"Maureen is a hero."

"Was," I sniffed.

"Is. She's still breathing. Barely...but she's alive," said Dorie, gently pulling away from me.

How?

I heard sirens and saw flashes of light. I could hear footsteps pounding toward us as police and medical personnel came streaming into the room.

"Save her...please!" Pointing to Maureen, I watched as a cleric began performing magical first aid. "Please save her...she's my friend."

Pandora raised her brows at this statement but shrugged and walked over to where Wilhelmina was curled into a ball. "This one, however, not so much. She's beyond saving."

Adriana joined Pandora and tsked, shaking her head at

what was left of her nemesis. "Wilhelmina, you old fool. What were you trying to accomplish?"

* * *

SEVERAL HOURS WOULD GO by before the police had everything sorted out and the medic could clear those who were well enough to leave. Nora wound up with an egg-sized welt on her head, a concussion, and a few days at the witch hospital. I brought her flowers and a few magazines and thanked her for coming to my family's aid.

"They're my family too, you ninny."

Yeah. We're still working on our relationship. We'd be fine. Nora would be too.

Maureen? Not so much. The young lady had weeks, if not months, of medical and magical treatment to reverse the vile sorcery that almost took her life. She was lauded as the heroine in our retelling of the night's events, and her hospital room overflowed with gifts and flowers.

She hasn't spoken a word.

Not in a coma but not reacting too much, Maureen sits silent. Vacant eyes stare out the window, and a listless countenance is all that remains of the fiery personality that was once my target. Now? Now I'd sit with her, read books, and brush her hair. I told her about the Fall Festival and brought her Halloween candy—just no spider decorations. We even watched scary movies...well, I watched; Maureen remained impassive.

It wasn't until I finished watching the last one and mentioned it was time for me to leave that I noticed a slight change. A lone tear ran down Maureen's face, and I quickly wiped it away. Then, I placed a chocolate lollipop in Maureen's hand—a tiny witch riding a broomstick—and leaned down close to whisper in her ear.

"I think it kinda looks like Adriana. Don't bite her head off and chew it up with too much elation, OK? Try to restrain yourself, my friend."

I couldn't be sure, but I think Maureen flashed me the barest hint of a smile.

I'd take that.

CHAPTER 23

I tried to enjoy my first real Halloween since I'd missed so many previously, Lorcan making sure to take me trick-or-treating as if I were a child. I dressed up as—what else—a witch. Only I sported vampire teeth as well.

Old Frank showed up with his pack. They all wore cute outfits to entertain the children. Rusty, looking well despite his illness, woofed when he saw me. Tail wagging, he came to rest his big, shaggy head in my lap while I enjoyed a caramel apple.

"I knew the minute you all fixed the sickness," said Frank. "Rusty's eyes cleared, and he began to bark...only this time with joy! Thank you." Reaching into his pocket, Frank pulled out a mason jar and handed it to me.

Moonshine.

I didn't have the heart to decline the illegal offering and quickly shoved it into my bag and thanked him.

The midday sun shone brightly over the festive town, and I tried to enjoy the sights and sounds even as a small group of people off in a distant churchyard caught my attention. I nodded in that direction, and Lorcan looked to where I'd indicated.

"They're burying Willie today." I sighed and tried to figure out how I felt about her death.

It was a lonely group. Cornelius, Boris, Stella, and Arthur stood huddled together in the small congregational church cemetery as their loved one was interred. I stood as a tiny figure dressed all in black strode across the lawn and joined them.

Adriana. Mending fences and offering comfort in her own way.

"Let's go home, Lor. I'm done."

"Good. I'm ready for that bonfire tonight," he replied.

* * *

AND WHAT A BONFIRE.

My family gathered at my place that night as the Halloween festivities raged onward. Everyone was here. Spirits were high despite the pall of Rowan Nightingale and her continued threat. We knew it would only be a matter of time before she resurfaced. Even after a massive countywide manhunt, no sign of the young witch was seen by anyone.

But she was out there, somewhere, biding her time.

Let her. I would wait. And next time? I'd be ready.

I watched as Pandora, dressed as a sexy devil—because really, what else would a crossroads demon choose as her Halloween costume?—danced around the fire, drinking from a paper bag Old Frank held out to her. Heck, he handed them out to all who wanted them.

I didn't fret too much about it. After all, Brian was holding one and draining its contents with Jake...so who was I to worry?

"Folks are getting rowdy," said Lorcan, laughing as

Pandora stoked the fire with Abner's favorite rake. Abner jumped up and down, trying to pull it back out, but up it went in an explosion of sparks. Ah, well...I'd have to buy him another.

"You want me to chase them all away?" I asked.

"Nah. Then I'd have to help, and I can't feel my legs."

"Lorcan Reid. Are you drunk?" I cried.

"And about to be disorderly, if only I can...no. I think I'll lie down right here and go to sleep," he replied. And he did.

Edith flew by, crashing into the bonfire, sending sparks in all directions. She was in a good mood despite them burying her grandmother today. To each his or her own. Edith deserved a bit of fun.

A few folks started a conga line, and Dorie hopped in the lead, taking them on a merry jaunt through my backyard, around the front, only to return to the warmth of the bonfire.

I felt someone slowly sit down to my left.

"Pandora is plastered," said Adriana.

"Drunk as a skunk. So's Lorcan," I said, hitching my thumb in his direction. The big oaf was already sawing logs.

"Anyone gonna tell Dorie she forgot her underwear again?" asked Adriana.

"Like you are one to talk," I cackled.

No. Wait. I don't cackle!

I watched as Dorie spun in circles to the delight of all the men present and sober enough to enjoy the show. Of course, they were probably seeing double if not triple of the cross-roads demon.

"Nah," I replied. "Dorie's having too much fun to go spoil it with underwear."

"Liliana Sweet. Have you been drinking?" barked my great-grandmother.

I snorted. "Maybe a little."

Now Grandpa Antonio joined Pandora, and he spun her around in a happy dance while everyone clapped and cheered. Andrea ran to Pandora with a pair of shorts, but Dorie tossed them in the fire.

The crowd roared even louder. I'm glad I don't have any side neighbors anymore. I watched as a black smoke trail rose into the night sky and I sobered a little.

"I know who it was," I said, turning to Adriana and locking my eyes with hers. "The inky shade."

"I figured."

"Lucretia. I guess I didn't quite finish her off that time. She must have slipped away."

"Yes."

"She's joined up with Rowan," I continued.

"Or she has been with her all along, Cara," said Adriana. "We don't know what happened there, but Rowan is mental. Totally unstable."

"I'm going to end her, you know," I said, meaning every word.

"One or both?" she asked.

"Both."

"I don't doubt it for a minute."

Jerry, my fairy godfather, ran past with both Max and Rex on his heels. He's finally made enough room for the hell-hounds to move in with him, and they were The Forbidden Library's new mascots—and guardians. Jerry couldn't be more thrilled because he's grumbled ever since he'd been displaced and the library moved to a more inviting location—for patrons anyway. Jerry didn't like just anyone to touch his children.

The man certainly had a thing for books, evening gowns, and shoes.

Only tonight he was dressed as, well...a man! I almost didn't recognize him in that fancy suit.

"Where's your gown?" I called out to him.

Indicating his outfit, he replied. "This is my costume. Armani. I'm here dressed as Jake!"

That lifted my spirits.

I glanced at Adriana, and we shared a laugh.

"Nora looks better. She has some color to her cheeks," said Adriana, noting my cousin's healthy glow.

"I'm glad she's out of the hospital."

"When will we have to explain everything to the Witch Council?" I asked.

Sheriff Glen, Brian, and Cornelius are working on the wrap-up now. They will present their finding at the next Elders meeting in mid-November. We will have the floor at that time," said Adriana.

"I want to air grievances."

"Sure. Whatever you want, Cara."

"And I want to announce to the world I have a magical talking cat. Where is Wicked anyway?"

"She was over by the Reids. Malcolm showed up, and he got to drinking with Henry. Didn't take long for Henry's dentures to fall out, and I think Wicked ran off with them," Adriana chuckled.

Poor Henry.

Poor Charlie. Dad was once again mentally frail. Adelaide is back to nursing him, and I watched as he sat on my back porch, away from the crowd with a slight smile on his face, although his forehead remained wrinkled. It would take some time to bring him back to where he'd gone.

My mom would get him there and keep him there. If anyone could do it, Adelaide could.

"It's a good party," I said.

"The best. Everyone who is anyone is here."

Except for poor Maureen. Here we are having fun, and

she's traumatized sitting alone at the hospital. I hated myself for all the ill will I'd ever sent her way.

I sighed and dropped my head.

"Maureen will recover. Give it time, Liliana," said Adriana, expertly reading my thoughts.

"It was all..."

"Don't even go there!"

"But..."

"No buts, young lady! It was not your fault!"

"It feels like it was," I mumbled.

"Liliana. Don't take that girl's act of bravery and make it something other than what it was," argued Adriana. "If anyone's to blame, it's Rowan."

"And Lucretia. Our kin. Our ancestor. Our responsibility. Why won't she go away and leave us alone?"

Adriana sighed, patting my knee with one gnarled, liver-spotted hand.

"Because she's evil. And evil knows no better. It eats her up and is the driving force behind everything she does. Even if she wiped every last one of us off the planet, still she'd find something to hate. And attempt to eradicate it as well."

"Only we won't allow it. We'll get to her first," I argued.

"Oh, we'll get her alright. You know we will. And do you know why?" asked Adriana.

"Because we're badass dark witches!" I cried.

"And don't you forget it. Now...help me up because I'm stuck."

"Sounds like you've been drinking too."

"Nah. I got dizzy riding around on my broom," Adriana replied with a cackle.

"There's no such a thing as a flying broom!" I argued.

"Yeah, yeah."

I watched her teeter off, heading over to Antonio and saving him from having to continue his raucous dance with

Pandora, who'd just chugged the rest of Jake's moonshine, tossing the jar into the bonfire.

BOOM!

Well, darn it. No one told Dorie Frank's moonshine is made of magic and mayhem. So now, how will we put out that fire?

Suddenly, Max ran over to the bonfire and lifted his massive leg into the air.

"No! Wait. Max. Stop it! Don't you dare..."

Too late. Especially when Rex came over and joined him. Nothing would get that fire relit after the dousing it just got.

Oh well, there's always next year!

CHAPTER 24

The next day I think everyone slept in until noon. I was confident all the local church officials were grumbling that Halloween fell on a Saturday this year.

I came downstairs to the smell of coffee and Lorcan sitting at my dining room table.

"Morning. What's this?" There was a gun on the table in front of my fiancé.

"Your weapon," said Lorcan. "Brian said you're clear to carry."

"But…a gun?"

"It's not an ordinary gun."

I stared at the sleek, cold metal, then peered up at Lorcan once more. "It sure looks like a real gun."

"Oh. It's real…but it's also magical. For humans or at certain times if you'll need it for Breed, it will fire bullets, silver bullets against vampires. But most of the time, it shoots stun magic…and worse."

I didn't know how I felt about carrying a weapon; my hands and magical misfires were weapons enough.

"Seeing as how you are Head Investigator for all things arcane, you are automatically licensed to carry."

"Without a mental evaluation?" I asked

Lorcan barked out a laugh. "Oh, well...then you'd never get to pack one," he teased.

Giggling, I leaned in for a quick kiss that turned into something a bit more serious. That has happened more often lately. Being in a battle to the death does wonders for your sex life. Coming up for air a few minutes later, I took stock of my new possession.

"This can kill Breed?"

Lorcan nodded yes.

"It would have come in handy with the Rowan situation."

"Only if she was truly there...and the jury is still out on that." Lorcan brushed some hair strands from my face and then tapped my nose.

"You couldn't save her, Lily. You can't save everyone."

"Wilhelmina had answers we needed."

My thoughts were interrupted by Wicked who pushed her way between us and meowed—loudly.

"Someone's hungry!" I laughed. "Do you believe me now? That I can hear my cat?"

"I didn't not believe you. It's just..."

'Weird, I know," I kissed Lorcan again despite Wicked sinking her claws in my pants leg.

"I'm going to get her, Lor. Kill her if I must."

"The cat?" Lorcan made a face of mock horror, and I laughed, then sobered.

"Rowan. I've marked her. I'm going to hunt her down and bring her in if I'm allowed."

"You are," he said. Lorcan sighed and searched my eyes. "Only you aren't allowed to die. I don't think the cat would like that. Or me."

"But I'm not a cop. So I won't constantly be out doing dangerous stuff."

"No, but you are like a magical private eye now," said Lorcan.

I smiled, and my tummy betrayed me by growling loudly. "Pizza?" I asked.

"Sounds good to me."

"I'll order." Standing, I retrieved the gun, feeling its bulk, then headed for the kitchen to find the menu for our pizzeria.

"Pepperoni?" I called out to Lorcan.

"Yeah…and pineapple," he replied.

I pointed the gun in his direction and shot him.

OK. No, I didn't. But I did spend a few seconds fantasizing about different scenarios of doing just that.

"There will be no pineapple on any pizza ever. Not in this house, mister! You got it?"

"Yes, ma'am!" I could hear Lorcan chuckling.

I wanted to remain upset. I should go back and read that man the riot act.

Pineapple!

I opened the junk drawer where I kept the takeout menus and glanced at the windowsill. Sitting between two of my potted herbs was a tiny pine cone. Undoubtedly the one Lorcan plucked from my hair on our lazy hammock day. He saved it. Another of his mementos tucked around the house to mark a special moment in our lives.

Yep. Definitely a keeper!

"Um, baby?" Lorcan shouted from the other room, "What about anchovies?"

Where are my bullets?

Thank you for reading! I hope you loved this latest Lily Sweet tale. Lily and the gang will return in Book 11 – Hell's Bells and Wedding Spells - and it's sure to be a wild ride.

I write in my own style that may not be everyone's cup of tea—so if you enjoy my characters and humor and are eagerly anticipating the next in the series, be aware that I am just as excited as you. THANK YOU!

I appreciate your help in spreading the word, including telling friends, family, coworkers…some random guy on the street. Reviews help readers find books! Please leave a review on your favorite book site by checking out my social media links on the next page!

Visit my official website to receive updates, find out about special offers and new releases, or read my blog about writing and farm life - complete with photos - you might even catch me mowing my ten acres (seriously): http://www.bettinamjohnson.net

To contact me:
author@bettinamjohnson.net

Sign up for my Newsletter: http://eepurl.com/gZKo51

Join my Facebook Group: Author Bettina M. Johnson's Team Wicked

For even more (if you just can't enough of me) and to LEAVE UNBIASED REVIEWS and catch my nutty posts...
follow my Social Media Links

tiktok.com/@bettinamjohnsonauthor

amazon.com/author/bettinamjohnson

bookbub.com/authors/bettina-m-johnson

goodreads.com/bettinamj

instagram.com/bettinamjohnson

facebook.com/authorbettinamjohnson

twitter.com/bettinamjohnson

AUTHOR BIO

I always knew I wanted to write. As a kid, way before the technology age had hit, I'd be stuck in the car with the folks as we drove from our home on Staten Island, NY, where I was born and raised, to our family property in the Catskill Mountains. To drive away boredom, I would sit, staring out the window, and create adventures of daring thieves riding horseback along the road, trying to escape the law. Other times I'd imagine a wild girl riding her unicorn into battle (I had a vivid imagination - we didn't have video games yet!)

As the years passed, I'd start writing a book, then stop, then start again only to let life get in the way, until one day I had an epiphany—a kick in the pants moment. If I waited any longer, all those wonderful characters in my head would never have their stories told, and that made me sad. So, I treated writing as my career. Once I started, it became apparent nothing would ever stop me again. YOU, dear reader, are stuck with me until I go off to that great library in the sky...or wherever writers go when they crumble to dust in front of their typewriters (or laptops...whatever)

I live in the North Georgia Mountains on what I like to

call a farm, with my husband, two sons, my daughter and my daughter-in-law, a Cairn Terrier named Fergus, Loki and Lily, my two black cats, and Lexi...our tuxedo cat who is put unadulterated evil.

Occasionally other critters show up to keep things exciting.

OTHER SERIES

And if you enjoyed Spells Like A Witch, you'll love Lily's cousins Maggie and Ellie, and their quirky, sometimes funny, sometimes dark, but always magical paranormal gang of monster-hunting antique appraisers. A Tale of Two Sisters, the tie-in series to my Lily Sweet World, highlights Lily's cousins Maggie and Ellie Fortune and is FREE on Kindle Unlimited!

> *"I am loving the snark in this book."*
> - S. Keller, BookBub author reviews.

And if two series wasn't enough, I'd like to introduce you to siren, Tarni Vanderzee in the first in the Secret Siren series: SIREN RISE. Refusing conformity. Embracing the unknown. Accepting what life throws her way over an oppressive past can bring Tarni ultimate joy...or total ruin!

There are even more series in the works! Two cozies: A Death on Demand Midlife Mysteries, and A Hire The Vampire Mystery.

And for you dark paranormal romance lovers: Night-shade and Necromancy will be a six-book series with plenty of spice and a strong female main character.

BOOKS BY BETTINA M. JOHNSON

The Lily Sweet Mysteries:

Home Sweet Witch

Witch Way is Up?

How To Train Your Witch

Sweet Home Liliana

Witch Way Did He Go?

Revenge is Sweet, Witch

Witch and Peace

The Sweet Spell of Success

I Spell Trouble

Sweet Briar Witch

Spells Like A Witch

Hell's Bells and Wedding Spells (Coming Soon)

* * *

The Fortune-Telling Twins Mysteries:

A Tale of Two Sisters

Double Toil and Trouble

Fire and Earth, Sisters at Birth

Kindred Spirits

A Djinn and Tonic

A Werewolf in Sheep's Clothing

A Pocketful of Pixies

No Kilt About It (Coming soon)

* * *

Secret Sirens

Siren Rise

Siren Star

Siren Fall (Coming Autumn 2022)

* * *

A Death on Delivery Midlife Mystery

Book 'Em, Danno

Trunk or Treat (Coming Soon)